Having spent most of his working life to date in education, a gradual rustication over recent years has given Ian greater opportunities to indulge in creative writing. It has also facilitated a coast-ward drift. Felicitously partnered, Ian shares most of his home with two witty beagles. *The Widowers* is his first published novel.

To Tassie and Lyka

Ian Carass

THE WIDOWERS

AUSTIN MACAULEY PUBLISHERS™
LONDON * CAMBRIDGE * NEW YORK * SHARJAH

Copyright © Ian Carass 2022

The right of Ian Carass to be identified as author of this work has been asserted by the author in accordance with section 77 and 78 of the Copyright, Designs and Patents Act 1988.

All rights reserved. No part of this publication may be reproduced, stored in a retrieval system, or transmitted in any form or by any means, electronic, mechanical, photocopying, recording, or otherwise, without the prior permission of the publishers.

Any person who commits any unauthorised act in relation to this publication may be liable to criminal prosecution and civil claims for damages.

This is a work of fiction. Names, characters, businesses, places, events, locales, and incidents are either the products of the author's imagination or used in a fictitious manner. Any resemblance to actual persons, living or dead, or actual events is purely coincidental.

A CIP catalogue record for this title is available from the British Library.

ISBN 9781398437005 (Paperback)
ISBN 9781398437012 (Hardback)
ISBN 9781398437029 (ePub e-book)

www.austinmacauley.com

First Published 2022
Austin Macauley Publishers Ltd®
1 Canada Square
Canary Wharf
London
E14 5AA

I have watched the local weather forecast three times now. Each time it says the skies are clearing and the sun will come out. But it's still raining, heavily raining, like some sort of festival for the gods of rain. Zeno looks at me, the way she can, the way you make believe that dogs can communicate on almost equal terms with us. She's asking when? When will the sun come out, when will the rain stop, when can we have our walk? I look at her, the way you do, the way you make believe they understand everything you want a look to say: I don't know, soon, soon.

Zeno is a dog, you will have guessed, and a female dog at that. And I know that the more famous Zeno who is her namesake was a chap and our Zeno is a girl. We liked the name that is all I can say. Yvonne liked the name.

See, I doubted I could get more than a few minutes into this before I said her name. It took less time than I thought.

She saw the name, Yvonne saw the name, Zeno, in some context or other; if she knew more than that, she never said. We had decided when we got Zeno that we wouldn't go for a person's name, like Fred or Maisie; that didn't feel right to either of us. But we really didn't spend much time actually choosing the name, when it came to it. Yvonne suggested Zeno and I agreed. I often just agreed like that. I didn't know then that Zeno had been a person, from some archaeological time, and a chap at that. It felt right for Zeno to be Zeno. It was different and distinctive and I knew I wouldn't be embarrassed calling out Zeno, Zeno, in the park or on the beach, if she ran off or was sniffing around a dead fish or a discarded kebab. No one, no person, would think I was addressing them, probably no other dog either, though I imagine it's tone rather than the words that dogs respond to. Maybe people too.

The name also had two syllables. I hadn't thought about it too much then but I realise now how useful two syllables are to nuance commands or emphasise chastisements. You can elongate the zee bit of it (Zeee-no) if you want to call her from far off. You can give it a staccato punch (Zee-no) if you want to stop her from doing something quickly. You can give it disappointment, exasperation, amusement, anger, comfort, all from the two syllables. You couldn't do that or not as readily I think, with one syllable (Rex or Flo) or even three syllables (Barnaby or Millicent). So it was a good choice, though now Zeno is cocking her head at me because I think I've tried out the inflexions for her name out loud.

I still don't know anything about the person called Zeno. Someone, not long after we had got her, tried to tell me about the historical Zeno but I stopped them. It was not relevant and I had rather not know. I didn't want anything to shape how I thought about her or her name. Now I think it might seem a bit disloyal to our Zeno if I looked him up. Daft, I know but I wouldn't want Zeno to think some long-ago chap had a sort of precedence. She's the genuine Zeno, unique and full of life and special. If Yvonne knew about that chap, what he did (general, poet, statesman or villain, whatever he was), she didn't tell me. If she saw associations that made the naming of the dog apt, I didn't find out. Maybe I should have asked, maybe I should have asked a lot of things. I haven't been one to question things too deeply. Increasingly now, I am more reflective. When you have time on your hands, you tend to think about things, I'm finding. I don't come up with conclusions from these reflections very often, just more things to think about but I'm suspecting that just accepting things at face value won't do anymore.

It didn't stop raining but we went out anyway. It was that drizzly kind of rain that often soaks you through more thoroughly than the stair-rods downpour. With the rain came a wispy sea-mist forming the kind of wet that gets under your collar and up your trouser-leg. Zeno bounded out, as usual, assailed with all those smells that fascinate and thrill them so much. That didn't last long. Soon she was dragging at her lead a bit and was damp as a dishcloth, looking up at me with her best expression of dismay. We persevered. There were no other dogs out, none of her pals, so nothing to take her mind off the rain, nothing to chase or sniff. A cyclist passed us and we got a good spraying all over us. Zeno growled a bit at that, unusual for her. I growled a bit inside too. I let her off the lead on the beach but she just clung around my legs, doing that shiver thing that I'm sure she can turn on or off as it suits her. She looked up at the sky now and then as if affronted and wasn't even tempted by a rotting fish, left beached by the tide. She did her business in a grudging way and then dug her heels in, mission accomplished, so we turned back. Even a break in the clouds didn't inspire her. I watched the clouds make room for a shaft of light (God's light, Yvonne called it) that illuminated the wind turbines way out at sea but nothing else. They stood out, clear as crystal, in a grey sea and a grey sky. These moments inspire and console me. Little glimpses of the wonder in the world, if we just stop to notice. I don't remember always feeling like this. I can't think of a time when Yvonne was alive when I was stalled in my footsteps to just look at something, admire it, and take it in. It happens all the time now. But I can't recall ever turning to her or her turning to me, to just point something out, to stand still and absorb it; a flower in the hedgerow, a quality of light or shadow. Maybe Yvonne was all the wonder in the world I needed then.

Zeno had given me a short bark (just the one syllable) and I saw her, waiting for me a little way off, wanting me to take her home and stop moping about.

I am back home and Zeno has had her rub down and got on the sofa, licking her paws to finish off the drying process. Dog hairs are everywhere. It was Yvonne's belief that we should train Zeno not to go on the sofa and chairs in the sitting room. Zeno was also banned from the bedrooms. I didn't object. This injunction worked all right for a while; Yvonne was strong on obedience training. But since Yvonne's death, I've let Zeno have free-ranging rights. Well, we live here together and I want her to be as comfortable as she can be. She's happy on the sofa, curling up on any warm spot that I leave whenever I stand up or snuggled into the crook of my arm when I watch television and she dozes off. Zeno still rarely comes upstairs, though. I wouldn't have minded a warm body beside me on the bed now and then but Zeno prefers her crate for sleeping. And I respect that. Maybe the bedroom is most where the scent of Yvonne still lingers. Maybe that olfactory reminder of Yvonne triggers the operation of the prohibitions that Yvonne drilled into her.

Most of Yvonne's clothes still share my wardrobe and there are a few bottles of her perfumes and such like about the place. Some things I threw away pretty promptly after Yvonne died. I didn't want her underwear around in the drawers (That felt a bit creepy); some of it looked a little surgical to me, with straps and buckles, not in the least what you might call sexy. Moisturisers and cleansers and that kind of thing (Not even sure what half of it was for) went in the bin. Some parts of the wardrobes and some drawers I haven't even looked in. As with most married couples, I imagine, the wife monopolises the hanging and storage space. If I ever found I needed more room for my things, I might end up having a purge but so far I have got rid of more of my own clothes than of hers. There were sweaters and shirts that Yvonne bought for me that I was always uncomfortable with and hated it when she laid them out on the bed for me to wear. Those went. I sometimes wonder if I'll encounter some chap wandering down the street in one of those shirts or jumpers after he has picked them up in a charity shop.

It's not exactly sentiment that stops me from throwing things away. I've never taken out armfuls of Yvonne's blouses and cardigans to get the last inhalation of her scent, as I've heard some people do. The clothes aren't important to me. At first, coming across stray hairs in the bed or a smudge of lipstick on a cup did upset me. It felt too immanent, too real, suggesting a presence that was no longer present. It was a phase of grieving, I suppose, that we all go through. Now, not having a clear-out is just a kind of laziness. The clothes aren't eating anything, as Mother used to say, so they can stay where they are. People might find it odd that I have kept them. Might imagine I am maintaining a shrine for Yvonne (Or worse that I might try them on in some sort of invocation). No one knows I have them still. No one comes here really, no one who would poke around in the bedroom, in any case. Her coats in the hallway went to charity, some of her books, that kind of thing. So she is less in evidence downstairs and in the more public areas. After she died, Yvonne's sister asked for the jewellery and I couldn't think of a reason not to let her have most of the stuff though I suspected it would be in the pawnshop or melted down by the end of the day. I haven't seen or heard from her since the funeral, to ask her. Those fake-Murano clowns that Yvonne was so fond of definitely went; first job after the funeral. I couldn't stand them. I didn't ever tell Yvonne that, of course.

It's mid-morning and I finally had a shower, shaved and had breakfast. Living by myself now, I have developed my own routines. I never found the knack for lying in bed once I am awake and I can be an early riser. Sometimes, from the perspective of five o'clock in the morning, the day in front of you can seem a long stretch of nothing, daunting and sometimes a little frightening. It doesn't usually pan out like that and by bedtime, I can often feel that I've never stopped all day, with one thing or another. I might even feel a little harassed or frustrated that I haven't found time to mow the lawn or buy bread or I've left it too late to walk Zeno properly. The day just takes care of itself and I never know where the time goes when I suddenly look up and see how late it has become. How the day gets filled up, I am never sure but it does always get filled, as it has to, I suppose. Little tasks, rituals almost, that used to take me twenty minutes when I was working now appear to occupy hours on end. Of course, I take little breaks between jobs. I will have a sit-down after I have put the kettle on, watch a bit of the news, and then find I need to boil the kettle again to make my tea. Now that the news is broadcast all day and all night, I find I can drop in and out of it and there's always something new happening somewhere. I think these days the 'news' is often just speculation or anticipation, telling you about things that might happen or are due to happen. Whether they do or not, you never find out. The big story one day you won't hear about again. Are the missing people ever found? Are the villains who stole something really important ever brought to justice? The breaking news stuff is quickly forgotten in favour of who is due to say whatever or go wherever (Did they, in the end, say it or go there, you are never informed). It's a discontinuous narrative, like the plots of those novels Yvonne was always trying to get me to read or the foreign films she liked.

I clean the house once a week, some areas more often, the kitchen every day. I follow Yvonne's regime in that regard. Yvonne worked all her life, well, till she went for early retirement. She was a primary school teacher. It could mean long hours some days, so she made it a rule from early on that we would share the housework and I agreed that it was only fair. She retired first but even after she had retired and theoretically had more time on her hands, I still did my bit. It wasn't something that I had been brought up to. Even at university, I would bring all my washing home with me, sometimes weeks' worth, for Mother. I never even touched an iron until I was in my twenties. Mother wouldn't have it any other way. Yvonne taught me the basics of ironing and I have applied my own style to it. I'm very thorough when I start something. So, I can sew a button on and iron a shirt, even though it probably takes me at least twice as long as it would someone who was born to it. Yvonne even trusted me with those flouncy, frilly blouses she liked, delicates, easily creased, needing a low heat and a deft touch. I can turn the oven on and the washing machine (Sounds daft but there are enough men who can't even get that far or say they can't). It comes over as boasting, doesn't it but it isn't or shouldn't be. Basic domestic chores shouldn't be beyond the wit of a man and it's not anything to be especially proud of that you can navigate a spin cycle or operate the defrost setting on a microwave. And there's no reason why it should be a woman's role to keep a household running. It was how we were brought up. It applied even in childless households. Whatever commitments she might have, she might even be earning more than the chap but he always expected his tea on the table. That's the way my father expected it and most of his contemporaries. Nowadays, I imagine both sexes learn domestic chores at the same time (Though deep-down, I doubt it). Perhaps neither sex does. According to Yvonne's sister, both my niece and my nephew were equally clueless when they went to university and had to do things for themselves for the first time.

I cooked as much as Yvonne did, perhaps more often, as she usually had marking or preparation or some such in the evening. I enjoyed it, mostly. Simple stuff mainly, meals that Mother used to make. Casseroles, corned beef hash, liver and onions, a bit of fish now and then, a roast at the weekend. Neither of us was big on puddings, so I never excelled at that side. I don't cook so much now. You never really bother to that degree when there's just yourself to see to. I try to eat healthily but I'm happy these days just to open a tin of soup and have it with a bit of toast. I'll stretch to an apple or a banana if I recollect my tally of the five a day.

To be fair, Yvonne turned her hand now and then to the garden and minor DIY but she always left mowing the lawn to me. She hadn't the patience with the edging and the fiddly bit around the apple tree; looked like the local rugby team had scrummed down on it sometimes after she'd had a go. But I didn't say anything ever. She could see the results as well as I could.

Yvonne always did the budgeting, though. Not sure how that happened. I dealt with budgets and finance in my job so you would have thought that it might have fallen to me but she kept that area to herself. She did it well or well enough. Bills got paid; there was money for holidays and treats. There's enough still in the bank, earning interest like it always did. I'll never spend it, however long I live.

Zeno has gone to bed early. I had dozed off on the sofa with the telly on and she had taken a hint and snuggled up in her crate. I'll lock up and go to bed, though likely won't sleep that well now.

I go to a local cafe for breakfast, one day a week, after Zeno has had her walk. It's something Yvonne and I did together and I am happy to maintain the tradition. It used to be a weekend when Yvonne was alive, usually a Sunday but I have found it gets a bit too busy for me then and I prefer mid-week, well I prefer Tuesday. It's always a Tuesday. The food can vary a bit; eggs a bit hard some days or a bit snotty, bacon a bit dried out. I keep going to the same cafe mainly because it's right on the seafront and if I can get my usual spot (And I can most

Tuesdays), there is a lovely view of the sea whilst you are eating; that vast, changeable expanse out there; grey some days, blue-green others, crashing waves or a calm to-ing and fro-ing. It always fascinates and engrosses. The number of times my food has gone cold, whilst I stare and stare, lost in thought. It wasn't like that with Yvonne (Though she loved the sea as much as I did, I think); she didn't like to linger over cooling food. She also usually had somewhere else to go afterwards, something to do, so didn't want me to dawdle.

There are a few regulars I see in the cafe. Some chaps seem to go in almost every day, have most of their main meals there probably. We say, good morning, maybe more. We each sit at our own tables, generally the same tables each time. I don't know their names, apart from Geoff, and that's only because I have seen him sometimes in other contexts. He has a dog and he is out with her around the same times as I am with Zeno. I have seen him at the gym too (Another tradition Yvonne began for me). I don't remember ever introducing myself to Geoff or he to me (Hello, I'm Paul stuff). I think I overhead his name spoken. The waitress in the cafe is good at getting the names out of people and using them often when she serves you. Part of her customer service I expect or a bit of mild flirting. I don't use Geoff's name when I say good morning to him, though. I have never received much attention from the waitress in the cafe, never encouraged it either, to be fair. So, I stay anonymous when I am there. I don't think, therefore, that Geoff knows my name.

There are couples who are regulars at the cafe too but they keep to the other couples who go like Yvonne and I did in our time. Single men, bereaved or unmarried, are not integrated with the couples. Loneliness, or aloneness, might be catching or contaminating, it seems. Even the couples Yvonne and I mixed with a little don't let on to me so much now that I am on my own. It's the other chaps I nod to and connect with at that simple level. We are all in the same boat, getting on with it as best we can.

You never see single women at breakfast in the cafe; some pairs or a group but no single women. They have better things to do. It's all part of the separate ways that men and women respond to bereavement, I think. We all know the statistics; it just seems part of the natural order that the men die first. It's a biologically determined rule that women live longer and cope better when they are left behind. Women are programmed to expect this and adjust to it. It is as if they have been acclimatising to the notion since early middle age. They have, ready-made their networks of friends, their routines and hobbies, set up in anticipation years before, and it's a smooth transition. The death of a spouse always comes as a surprise to the men. It's not something we expect to happen; we have no structures to deal with it, no mental architecture to accommodate it. We are lost, alone, isolated. Nothing in our lives can replace it. We keep up old routines and even begin new ones but it's a drop in a void. Men shouldn't survive their wives.

I see the lost men – and I'm one of them – making the journey to the paper shop every morning (And sometimes every afternoon too). They are always too early, standing there waiting for the shop to open, muttering in a good-natured way about how the shopkeeper has been late opening up every morning this week. They have already spent an hour or so shaving, showering and making the bed. There is a little bit of conversation between the men, always the same, the weather mainly. They stamp their feet a bit on a frosty day, loosen a button if it's set to be warm. And off they toddle, back home, paper under their arm. It can take all day to read it. Maybe the crossword lures them in first, maybe the TV guide, rarely the headlines. What on earth would headlines matter to them now? If they have bought the local paper, it is the deaths and obituaries that they turn to first.

The mix in the knot of faces changes from time to time. Old faces disappear. Sometimes temporarily, returning with a stick or beneath their shirts and jackets that cross-hatching of stitching scars down their chest, that you see on some of the old-timers in the gym. Sometimes they don't ever return and the group closes by a degree for a time. New faces appear and are relatively quickly assimilated into the group if they want to be.

If they have children, these men, they are not nearby. A daughter or a son might have left the grandkids with them for a week or so over the summer in the past but since mum died, they feel it's too much for Dad to deal with. The children are growing up, the boys can be a handful, and the girls have nothing in common with him. Dad can barely look after the house and himself these days, let alone cope with children. He is becoming set in his ways too; he can be grumpy and is uncomfortable with changes to his routines. Of course, they ring him up every week, every month, at Christmas or whenever, to check on him, he seems to be fine, never complains or gives them cause to worry.

It's not all like that, I'm sure. I am aware that I am generalising too much from a few cases I know of. I don't want to sound bitter or negative or anything. I know many men manage well enough; I manage well enough. Some must thrive and have a fulfilling retirement, building pond yachts in the shed, taking up photography or water-colouring, being active in the church or on committees or at the golf club. It's just that it's not generally something I see. Only that sense of living in the aftermath. It starts as a dream, to retire to the seaside like a permanent holiday but you can end up feeling shipwrecked and marooned. The sun does not shine every day, the winters are still as cold, the rain pelts down and a withering wind keeps you indoors all too often. At the end of a holiday, we all say we will stay in touch but how many of us do, after a lapse of time or distance?

Today is a Tuesday and as I have explained, on Tuesdays I go to the cafe. Breakfast is over with now, I am back home and maudlin musings packed up for today. As is my general rule, after breakfast at the cafe I will stroll into town and pick up a few things. I did not get much this morning; it was more about stretching my legs than needing anything in particular from town. The items I did buy have been packed away and I have let Zeno out into the garden. I am due a sit-down.

We are lucky here in that there is still a good range of local shops, the kind that you used to have in every high street, a butcher (In fact, two butchers), a greengrocer, a baker. Being a seaside town, there are also takeaways and those daft sweetshops with rock and candy dummies and jars of bottled boiled sweets. Shops selling things that people only buy when they are on holiday. They all seem to make a living. Out of season, several shut up shop or at least cut their hours.

I tend to stick to a regular shopping list of items when I pop into town through the week. At the butchers, I will buy a few chops, that Zeno and I will share, mince (To cook in one of two ways), some boiled ham, sausages and a pork pie. A few obligatory bits of veg and fruit from the grocer, a loaf from the baker, maybe a cake, and that will see me through for most of the week. I will do a bigger shop at the supermarket, a short way out of town about once a month. The corner shop meets all my other needs. There are certain items less easy to get on the parade of shops but I prefer to shop as locally as I can. Some weeks, not every week, I will have fish and chips on a Friday, two large haddocks, one is for me. It is certainly the best fish I have ever had anywhere but that could be just the sea air and eating it hot from the fryer.

After shopping this morning, I walked back along the front. It was a beautiful morning, cold but everywhere glittering under unaccustomed sunshine, the sea a great plate of blue. Zeno would have been getting impatient for my return but there was a seal in the bay, close enough to see its whiskers, and I couldn't help but watch him for half an hour or until he swam off. I had saved a bit of sausage from breakfast and Zeno forgave me for dawdling, quickly enough.

Last night was a bit stormy and I didn't sleep well. Zeno does not like thunder and lightning and there was a bit of whimpering. In the end, I got up and let Zeno out of her crate and we sat on the sofa together. It reassured her. I had a cup of tea but didn't put the telly or the radio on or anything. We must have sat just quietly together for a couple of hours. Not another peep out of Zeno, apart from a bit of snoring and once that twitchy eye-rolling thing she does when she is very deep in sleep, her legs thumping away, dreaming of chasing rabbits across an open space, I imagine. Do all dogs do this? I don't know. I have never had a dog before.

I suppose I was thinking again, as the rain battered the windows and you could hear the swell of the sea. I was thinking of the time we first moved here. We passed the anniversary of our moving date a week or so ago and I suppose it has been on my mind. The coming summer will be my seventh summer season; Yvonne was with me for only three of those summers. It is a long enough period for me to have associations here, to find traces of Yvonne in familiar streets and points throughout the town, places where we ate, places we visited, little neglected areas of the coast we felt we discovered together. A few of those places I avoid without thinking about it. There are other places that were so ingrained into our daily life that I could not cut them out without limiting my life. Some spots I might come upon unexpectedly and suddenly remember that I had been there with Yvonne. On occasions, I seek out somewhere with special associations. I will walk along the cliffs to find that viewpoint we enjoyed and remember her. There are days when you want to remember and days when you want to forget.

It was a day towards the end of February when we moved in and it was snowing a bit. We had no idea what a summer season would be like, packed with tourists or just a little bit busier. Arriving here just in the final weeks of winter, the town was quiet. There was a community still in evidence but signs too of hibernation. Some shops were closed, others only had limited opening. Walking Zeno on the beach, days on end, we would not meet a soul.

The thing that struck me most coming here was the night. It was so dark and the sky was full of stars. You forget living in a town what a star-lit sky really looks like. We didn't come from any big city but it still had well-lit streets casting that orange glow everywhere, obscuring the skies. There are fewer streetlights here but it is that great black gulf of the sea that makes the difference. No lights out there apart from a few ships, tankers or trawlers, I am not sure but big ships on the horizon. They are far enough out that during the day you cannot see them apart from sometimes on the clearest days but at night, the lights they show pick them out. It was so dark that neither of us could sleep and we had to get a little night light for the landing just to see our way to the loo. Outside at night, looking up you got dizzy. You focused on one group of stars and then as you adjusted to the vastness, you could discern a group behind them, then another, until it seemed a huge, milky mess of stars, receding to infinity with a massive moon beaming out at its centre, its light a shining path across the sea.

Yvonne had retired before me. Over the years, Yvonne had suffered from a few health problems and she had quite a bit of absence from the school where she worked on that account. I got the impression though that there were also people problems at work. Some folk she just seemed to rub up the wrong way and it's pretty unpleasant when one of them is your boss, the Headteacher, David, I think he was called. Yvonne didn't discuss a lot of this in detail. Once I found her crying at home and she told me a little of what was going on for her. I said then, straight away, if you aren't happy, just leave. I didn't get into the rights or wrongs (You've got to assume that your wife is in the right in these circumstances, haven't you), I just wanted to be supportive. I suggested that she look for another job, move to a different school. She had been at the same school all her working life, had not been promoted at all. She never seemed to have sought advancement or extra responsibilities but I imagine it can rankle seeing younger folk, less experienced, coming in, promoted over your head. A change, I thought, would be good for her but her sense of loyalty and dedication kept her there, I suppose.

Yvonne did leave the school in the end but not for a while after the problems she had hinted at. Some good deals on early retirement eventually came up and then she jumped at it. She was lucky. Those deals were not, and will not, ever be repeated, I suspect, so she picked a good time to go, whilst she still had the vigour to enjoy retirement. I think she was ready for it and had more than done her bit.

Odd thing that I have just recalled, mentioning his name brought it to mind. I am almost sure that I saw that David in Cornubay, a couple of months ago. I only met the man two or three times, at school or teacher social things but I was pretty convinced it was him; still had that beard but grey now. I could be wrong but it's not that unusual to see people up here you have known or knew of from long ago. It is a seaside town, after all, folk from all over come to visit. If he recognised me, he didn't let on, didn't show a flicker. I wasn't about to greet him (If it was him, and I couldn't be sure), after his history with Yvonne at the school. We just passed on the street. He was with a woman, his wife, I assume.

I did not retire until about four or five years after Yvonne. My employer was seeking to make savings and offered its more senior staff a deal. It was not such a good deal as Yvonne's, my pension would be reduced but it meant that I did not have to keep working until my state pension kicked in. Yvonne and I agreed we could easily get by. We had no mortgage, we had some savings, so we would be fine. By the time I retired, Yvonne had her life sorted out. She was a member of a local amateur dramatic group, she was a governor at a school (Not the one she had taught at), had day trips out with friends and lunch dates a couple of times a week, had taken evening classes and was in a reading group. I more or less had to fit in around this, when my time came round. Someone once told me that it takes about a year to get used to being retired. I think it took me longer.

I have been asked a few times if I missed work and working. I always say no, I couldn't wait to leave but there are aspects of it that I do miss, the structure it gives you, the reason it gives you to get up in morning, the framework that underpins the comings and goings of your day. By the time I retired, I suppose I had achieved a certain status and earned the respect of colleagues. Those, probably artificial, indicators of position and worth disappear when you retire. Some seek to replace this standing through a community role or similar. I never did, never thought I would miss that aspect of working life but I did a little.

Though I never saw it as a competition, it gave me some satisfaction when I was finally earning more than Yvonne. Ultimately, I was earning a good deal more than her. I might have felt slightly that this should have given me a bit more kudos than it seemed to do in the home. At work, I was listened to, my advice was sought, and my opinion mattered. Before I retired, I directly managed a team of about twenty full-time staff, supplemented by a floating team of part-time staff. I interfaced directly with senior school and community staff, governors and councillors. My role covered a wide area: academic standards, committee work, and funding and education policy. I was quite a different person at work, I think; a little more confident and assertive than I was or have been in any other sphere of my life. Of course, a lot of this comes from longevity and being well-briefed and well prepared, hard work and persistence, in other words. But I have a very good organising mind and can frame an argument when required to. There must have been people skills in the mix too, communication skills, a certain degree of decisiveness. Why I discovered or uncovered these skills only past the mid-point in my career, why I couldn't transfer them to other areas of my life, why they seemed so absent or in abeyance in my youth, are questions I sometimes return to. Experience, I suppose. It gives you the nous to present as the thing you want to be. Not that I was quaking with fear every day. It wasn't just a front. Inside I was that person too. But just in that role in my life, it seems. When I left work, I left all that behind. And no one is indispensable. I know that, and if I didn't, I soon discovered it. There were no phone calls from my successor or former colleagues seeking my input on a difficult decision or advice on a thorny staffing or logistical problem. I put this down to the comprehensive notes I prepared when I left, the meticulously maintained systems and well-kept files. Or just that people felt I deserved a well-earned rest and it would be wrong to disturb me or draw me into something I had left well behind. I did, however, dread hearing through the grapevine that the department had been restructured and most of what I had put in place had been cleared away before my desk was even cold. I don't think that did happen or if it did the grapevine did not stretch as far as me.

It is fair to say that for at least six months after retiring, I had something like withdrawal symptoms. I am sure everyone feels an element of this, taking leave of what has been the better part of your life. I was not career-minded or ambitious in an obvious way. I was promoted internally, in the normal course of things but never applied for a job away from the council. I was always grateful for that first opportunity they gave me, setting me on when I had almost begun to despair. That alone creates loyalty.

If Yvonne and I had retired at the same time, I think we would have found our way together but I felt like a spare part when I was finally put out to pasture, under her feet, hanging about the house. I wondered if half the stuff she took on, her courses and her days out, was just to have time away from me. Maybe I seemed a bit needy and she did not want the responsibility of keeping me busy or entertained. Like her, I needed to find my own life in retirement. I don't think I ever did, quite. This is probably when the idea of a dog came into play; company for me and occupation of sorts. At least that bit worked out well.

We did still have our holidays together, more than we used to, when we both were retired. Despite her artistic and cultural interests, Yvonne was not one for going abroad. We had tried it but she didn't like the heat or all the organising it took or even the food. She said she missed home and her friends but I think at bottom, she hated flying, had a fear of the airport, the checking in, the being unsure where to go and what to do, the lack of familiar things and facilities about her, the language issue, fear of being ripped off by taxi drivers and restaurants, fear of falling ill abroad. There was a long list, all prefaced by the word 'fear'. She found herself in an environment that she couldn't control or predict, in the way she could at home. It's not too surprising, it scared me too but I felt less fear when we were together. I knew we could face whatever was thrown at us. It was worth it too, seeing all those wonderful sights, great art, beautiful churches, castles and cathedrals, plus I really enjoyed trying new food. Perhaps, Yvonne didn't feel she could rely on me for support whilst we were away, in the way that I felt with her. Perhaps she thought ordering food and finding places, asking for directions, fell too much to her. It did in a way but then, why did she spend all those years learning French and Italian at evening classes if she didn't want to use her skills when she visited those countries?

I think if we had been accustomed to going abroad growing up, as the young people seem to be today, we would have thought nothing of it. We were both in our forties when we first went. Yvonne and I came from a small town, our parents had not travelled much, had never been abroad. None of their friends had either, apart from those who were old enough to be shipped off to the continent and further afield during the war. My parents eventually went on a Spanish package holiday late in their retirement and always said after that they wished they had gone sooner. As children, we never had holidays anywhere but in this country, and then we never travelled very far from home. Even going to university felt like embarking on a trip to navigate the Northwest Passage. Like Rome, our hometown was surrounded by seven hills and it took a spirit of fearless adventure to scale them. The local railway station had two railway tracks. On one platform was a sign that said, 'Liberford and beyond', on the other platform the sign read, 'Carriefield and beyond'. These two places were the two closest towns. To me, it felt like the 'beyond' bit of these railway signs was like the watery edges on old maps, here be dragons. The boundaries of our world were narrow and forbidding; you were likely to drop off the edge of the world if you ventured too far. No wonder foreign travel felt like launching into space.

Yvonne and I visited many places in this country over the years. We always stayed by the sea, never inland. It didn't feel like a holiday if we could not see the sea every day, preferably from every window. I think we were at our happiest at those times. There was just the two of us, we only had each other for company (Until Zeno entered our lives) and we turned back towards each other. We grew closer, sharing that time exclusively, planning what to do and where to go. In the interest of frankness, I should also say that the physical side of our marriage was rekindled on those holidays (I don't think that this is uncommon). It was not much more than a pilot light back home.

We usually booked a little cottage, so our privacy was complete. We shopped for the few things we needed together, cooked and ate together. Yvonne was there just for me; no night classes, no meetings, no brunches with her friends. These were wonderful times and I just hope that Yvonne felt the same way about our time together on those holidays. To me, it was always too short a time. Yvonne sometimes seemed to get a bit restless towards the end of the holiday. I wanted to bring that holiday spirit back home with us but it did fade once we were in the old routines and that little bit of strangeness between us crept back in.

Yvonne must have felt something of the joy of those little holidays because it was she who first suggested that we move to the coast, as our final home together. At that stage, it was only an idea and several general locations were under consideration. We came to a decision after we stayed at a place just up the coast from here. It was nice enough but Yvonne's sister, who lived not too far away inland, recommended that we visit Cornubay whilst we were in the area. I think we fell in love with it as soon as we arrived. It seemed perfect. It was close to Yvonne's sister, there were lots of amenities; there was even a cottage hospital in the town. Cornubay is also only about twenty miles from Canton, which is a fair-sized town, not quite a city, with an art gallery, theatres, cinemas and all the big shops. The town was pretty, housing was not expensive and it had a railway station, linking to the rest of the county, most of all though, it was the sea that drew us. The cliffs embracing the yellow sands, the way the tide seemed to go out for miles, the little, painted pier.

I hardly dared hope that Yvonne would agree to a move to Cornubay as our retirement home. I did not think for a moment that she would want to leave all her friends and groups and hobbies behind. I thought they mattered a lot to her. But it seemed she had wanted to be closer to her sister for a while. My impression was that they did not always get on that well (They were very different) but family is family, I suppose, and Yvonne had always been fond of her sister's children. Yvonne did also hint that she was a bit bored with the amateur dramatic set, saying that factions had developed. She was ready for a change of scene, something of a new start and a break with people and places that had become rather dreary.

I should have guessed that Yvonne had already done her research and internet searches in preparation for the move, there was a lot going on that Yvonne would fit right into. There was an amateur theatre group, in particular, that Yvonne would want to join, and there were many nice cafes and restaurants and bars. So when Yvonne told me that she was happy to agree to a move to Cornubay, she had already made sure it would suit her. I don't think she looked up woodworking or golf courses or sea angling, things that I might have conceivably taken up; she knew I wasn't one for clubs. I was very, very happy to accept the proposal. I had that optimistic feeling that we would replicate our holiday bond here. I think we did too, for a time, a time that proved all too short.

Once we had set our minds on the place, we came here every weekend and Yvonne sometimes on her own, to look at houses. She wanted a place that was central, with the shops within walking distance, and the seafront about the same. Yvonne found this place when she was here by herself. It was a larger than average semi, with three bedrooms, a garage and off-street parking. It was well-maintained, well located and according to the estate agent's details, well-loved and well-maintained (That at least stretched the truth a little bit). It had a large garden too, which is a bonus in coastal towns, I think and great for Zeno. Yvonne was keen not to lose the property and I was happy to trust Yvonne's opinion without viewing it myself. I didn't actually see the place until the day we moved in but I had seen the estate agent's details and couldn't fault it. We put an offer in the day after Yvonne viewed it and with a little bit of the usual haggling, the offer was accepted. Our own house sold reasonably quickly and we moved up here about six months later. We got a good price on our old house. The new one was a good bit cheaper, so we even had a nice nest egg left over.

Of course, Yvonne plunged into community life from the start. Very soon she was organising things and managing things and attending things. We saw Yvonne's sister and her family from time to time. Yvonne went over to see her sister every week and I am glad they became a bit closer again. Friends (Yvonne's friends) came over to stay now and again, at least in that first summer. The spare bedroom was the first room we did up. After that, our enthusiasm for decorating waned a little, and since Yvonne died, I haven't done a thing to the house. I think it will stand up for as long as I do. A little maintenance here and there should make sure. But Yvonne was the one with the flair for decoration and soft furnishing. I wouldn't know where to start, to be honest.

Zeno wants her breakfast and I will have a bit of toast with her. I am feeling a bit low today, I realise. The weather makes you want to just huddle by the hearth. On a day like this, Zeno will be content to just nip outside into the garden for her business. If it brightens later, we will go for a walk. If not, I will at least take her to the park this evening, stretch her legs and mine. I will try not to get too maudlin. But there is nothing I have to do, nothing that can't wait. I'll sit here for a while. I'll put the news on.

The week brightened as it went on and Zeno and I have shaken off a bit of the lethargy that had got into our bones, like the cold. She isn't a young dog anymore and I want her around and fit for a good few more years, so I shouldn't encourage her to sit on the sofa all day. It's not good for me either. I start to recognise the curve of that spiral that takes you down when you dwell too much on the past and eventually start to see only grievances, regrets and disappointments in your life, starting with childhood. It isn't healthy and I hope, it isn't a true picture. My life hasn't been all gloom, by any means. Zeno picks me up from these moments, usually. She puts her paws up on my knees as I sit in my old dressing gown, probably staring into space. She either wants feeding or a walk or just a bit of my wandering attention. Today, we'll have a long breezy walk on the beach. There's a freshness in the air and a bright early spring sun. On these clear days, you can see the lighthouse on the headland. You see it at night, of course, that striding beam strobing the sea, a warning but most likely for some a sign of home close by.

    I let Zeno off the lead on our walk this morning and away she went, bounding ahead of me as if she had never seen a beach before in her life. Everything is new. Sometimes when she is full of adrenaline or just that spirit of freedom and possibility that the empty beach gives you, she will run and run, shaking off the years. You can see the puppy in her still. That spirit stirs a little in me too, though it doesn't inspire me to chase after her. She always avoids the sea, directly. Zeno loves to jump into still water, splash about in shallow pools but moving water, water that chases her, she won't go near. In some ways, it is a bit of a relief. I never fear that she is one of those dogs you hear about that ventures too far out, or gets caught out by a freak wave, and her daft or devoted owner goes in after her and they both end up drowned. Eventually, Zeno will run out of puff and sit up ahead of me, tongue lolling, panting heavily, till I catch up with her. She will then stick close by me as we head home.

I bumped into Geoff on the walk back. He was just starting out. I don't know what breed of dog he has, a small dog, it's a bit hyperactive, friendly but seems to have a bit of a screw loose and doesn't always come back to his command. I am not that knowledgeable about dog breeds or their characteristics. I can recognise Labradors and poodles, that's about it. There are so many types of crossbreeds and mixes that appear to be fashionable these days that I don't bother to get better informed. Really, Zeno is the only dog that matters to me. She is a friendly dog, always wants to say hello to other dogs, and she will play with them, if they are up for it, despite her getting on a bit in years now. I really don't understand those owners who keep their dogs on a tight leash, drag them away from other dogs, seem to make it a fault in discipline if their dog responds to other dogs and wants to do the bottom sniffing thing. No wonder those dogs can end up a bit timid or a bit nasty when some pup bounds up to them, not knowing any different. I am no canine expert, have only Zeno to measure dog behaviour against but it seems unnatural. Dogs are pack animals, social animals. They bond by scent and if you deny them that natural route of communication you effectively ostracise them and it damages them, I think. I don't like dogs jumping up too much or being out of control, however, some discipline is required, they need to recognise boundaries and know who is boss. They say dogs reflect the personalities of their owners and you can be sure that some grumpy old git, who doesn't give you the time of day, is likely to have a grumpy old dog who at best ignores other dogs, at worst gives them a bit of a low snarl if they get too close. Not sure what that analysis says about me.

Zeno and Bella (Geoff's dog) sniffed about a bit, Bella rolling onto her back, paws in the air and belly exposed. Zeno kept a bit of distance today, for some reason. Probably put off by Bella's belly display antics, as I was slightly. It seemed too exaggerated, a show of submission. Geoff and I exchanged greetings and complimented the weather. It looked like he might want to chat for longer but I had things to do so made my farewells soon enough.

Zeno and I have no plans for the day but a few little jobs have accumulated whilst we were in hiding. I have been sorting through the post that has come. Yvonne still gets stray letters, even now. I think I informed everyone official about her death, pretty soon afterwards. The last thing you can be bothered with after a death, really but you get around to it in good time. I assumed that her sister got in touch with family members who would want to know, even if they hadn't been in touch for years. Yvonne had a wide range of friends, some she distantly kept in touch with, with postcards and Christmas cards, some closer but most of them I had no idea how to contact. Her phone gave a few clues but after only a couple of calls, I gave up on that. One was a near-stranger, who had almost no idea who I was talking about. One was the plumber. Another other kept me on the phone for an hour, unburdening all her memories of Yvonne. I didn't feel that I could face any of those types of calls again. I felt I should let people know about the funeral and I made the effort as best I could, becoming more selective in who I tried to reach. The friends that I knew as being close to Yvonne I did contact and asked them to pass the news on to anyone they knew who would want to come.

Not many did make it to the funeral. Whether I didn't make enough effort at this, I don't know. Perhaps they didn't get the message or did and couldn't face it. We are a bit out on a limb here. I didn't offer to put anybody up, so it could have seemed a long round trip for some. Many of our friends and family are getting on in years. I can see it wouldn't be a journey they would want to make. Someone had suggested I should hold the funeral in the town where we used to live, so more people could say goodbye. I suppose I could have done that but Cornubay was our home, my home, and I had severed that last link to our old home.

It was always going to be a cremation. There is a small stone memorial in the local church here, containing her ashes. I visited almost every week for a year or so but then I gave up. What was the point really? I thought it would be a focal point for my memories of her but we had not been regular churchgoers and the spot where she lies is a bit dreary, around the back, with a run-off from the roof guttering. It's damp and unwelcoming. Sometimes drinkers hang around there. Yvonne wasn't there; I'm not sentimental that way. It depressed me to go.

So, infrequently, a letter or card comes for Yvonne. With official-looking things, letters from charities or department stores or whatever, if they have a return address, I send them back, marked 'deceased'. They have gradually fallen off. Personal stuff I tend to open now. If I recognise the name or there is an address somewhere in the letter or card, I will usually try to contact them to let them know that Yvonne is gone but I don't strive too hard. If they haven't heard about her death by now, they can't have been that close or important to her. Last week there was a letter from an old school friend. I remembered that person vaguely. Had no idea Yvonne was in touch with her (Enough at least to let her know that we had moved to the coast and to give her that address). There was a small reference to me in the letter, that I found a bit unpleasant, some recollection she had of me from school and how unlikely our getting together and staying together all those years had seemed to Yvonne's friends. Everyone had wondered at the time if she was on the rebound, if she was trying to make 'a certain person' jealous or there was some other 'trouble'. The 'gang' (Whoever they were) all missed her and wished Yvonne would come back home. Even Freddy was very sorry she had moved away. I had no idea who this Freddy person was. I didn't like the tone of the letter or the speculation it contained. I was sure that Yvonne did not know the letter writer well and there was some mischief in the approach. However, I didn't dwell on all this, just tore the letter up and binned it. I think most future correspondence for Yvonne might go the same way, unopened. I don't want anyone outside spoiling my memories.

Yvonne and I had met at school but not until the sixth form. We lived in different parts of the town, attended different schools, and our paths had not crossed before that time. The two high schools in the town fed into one sixth form college. The number of children staying on beyond O level was so small that the town could only sustain one institution for A level study. It could be a bit competitive for that reason. I think I did just well enough to scrape in and Mother had encouraged me to stay on when it looked as if my examination results were likely to qualify me for consideration. Yvonne and I did not have dissimilar backgrounds, well nobody did, in that town. Yvonne's family was a little better off than mine or lived as if they were. Their home was in a slightly 'better' area. This does not say much really, as the degrees of affluence across the whole town fell within a pretty narrow range, even if vigorously cherished and strictly demarcated by those who benefited from a few extra pounds of income or a superior class of dwelling or environment. Yvonne's father had a garage and he sold cars, a business that had been in the family for a couple of generations. Her mother didn't work and never had, having married her husband straight from school. My father worked for the Co-op, in the insurance department. Mother had worked in a dress shop in town, part-time, until it closed down when the big department store opened. She had given up work when I was about eleven. Her period of employment, she always said, wasn't for the money but for the company.

In the sixth form, Yvonne and I had shared a couple of classes together and must have perceived a flicker of attraction or interest. We got on, discussed our essays and revision preparation. Sometimes we went for walks or to the cinema.

It was all a bit different, if rather innocent. I had never had a girlfriend before and she had not had a boyfriend or so I understood. We didn't use those terms to describe us but we did more or less acknowledge when it was asked, that we were courting, as the old folk quaintly called it. At the end of the sixth form, we might have gone our separate ways, we had no plans beyond that time, had no idea how to progress things. We had a bond but it wasn't a burning flame of passion or anything. What changed it was that Yvonne wrote a letter to me after our final school term ended. It was just a chatty note really, asking how I was, what plans I had, whether I had found a summer job. People did write letters in those days. Neither of us had a phone at home and letters were the only option to maintain contact with someone. Living a distance apart in the town, there was not likely to be any occasion for us to meet again. I replied and in due course, we met for a coffee. We had only a few brief months in that summer between school and college to get to know each other properly. It was quite intense at moments.

It was largely a long-distance relationship in the early years. We were at different colleges; me at university and Yvonne at teacher training college. We were only two counties apart but the distance thing seemed much greater then, with our small-town mindset. I imagine it is only about an hour and a half by car but in those days, it would have been three buses and a train journey. Not insurmountable, of course, and we did make the occasional forays, she to me, me to her but generally, we exchanged letters to keep the flame alive. Infrequently, with a lot of organisation, we spoke on the phone. Yvonne had access to a phone in her hall of residence, me at a callbox down the road. If there was a queue at the callbox or our timings were just a bit out, we could easily miss each other, with the phone ringing and ringing in Yvonne's hall or some stranger picking it up, when Yvonne had finally despaired of me getting through. I would trudge back to my student house in the rain, disconsolate.

We had the summer each year back home to share, between any holiday jobs we had and on-and-off studying. Long walks into the countryside. A lot of cinema visits and so on. Neither of us drank alcohol much in those days, so pubs were not really our thing, and we hadn't a great deal of money to spend on entertainment. A meal out was totally out of the question.

As we were so often apart, I think we both half-expected or half-feared that the thing might fizzle out or in the course of three years, a more local interest supervene. By which I mean, she or I might form an attachment elsewhere. It wasn't an option for me, I think. I certainly didn't look for it and I don't recall any serious offers or even any sustained overtures or indications of attraction coming my way. It might have been different for Yvonne. She was a pretty girl. I didn't enquire and she didn't mention. I know that the college had a predominantly female student body and that could have been a factor in her fidelity. At any rate, we survived those years, even thrived, I think.

Letters can be very intimate things, I feel, very personal. It's a lost art now, you might say. Even then, not everybody had the patience to write letters and I remember all too often that immense feeling of disappointment or frustration when a letter you had spent hours getting just right and filling with all your latest news and a few amusing snippets went unanswered. Lost in the post, overlooked, ignored, you could never know the fate of a letter, how it was received or interpreted, until or unless you got a reply. A short reply to a long letter was almost as bad as no reply. A few hasty lines with a promise to write more later (A promise rarely kept) could leave you feeling deflated, spurned or vaguely offended. Yvonne and I exchanged letters throughout our years apart. It was the only sustained correspondence I had with anyone over that time, the only one that survived to the end of my studies. One or two old school friends wrote to me initially and I replied diligently but they all petered out. I soon lost interest in keeping up a stream of communication by post, when nothing much was flowing back the other way. Even my parents and my sister didn't write to me beyond my first term or so. Well, terms were relatively short and I was always back home for vacations. I could see how it might not seem worth the bother but I would have enjoyed the odd letter now and then.

College ended. Somehow three years didn't seem that long a time. The final year seemed to go by in a flash. I suppose we were both working hard, in anticipation of the final exams. I was never an outstanding student. I wasn't a bad student either. At school and at university, I always fell in the middle somewhere; neither excelling nor failing conspicuously, not attracting any attention, not winning any prizes, unless it was for attendance. Somehow, I always did rather better than expected when it came to a test, an exam or some crucial piece of work. The big occasions perhaps inspired me to work extra hard. Or perhaps I had been underrated by my teachers and peers, never consciously seeking the limelight of praise or approval. Mostly I think you have to be a bit flashy to do well in life, push yourself forward, gain promotion and recognition.

Though sometimes, just getting your head down, working hard and sticking at it can work as well.

So, consistent with past form, I did rather better in my finals than was expected; Yvonne's results must have been a bit disappointing for her. I think the pressure got to her a little but we both passed and had to move forward to join the world of work. Yvonne's path was pretty much mapped out for her by her choice, of course, mine was a bit vaguer and more uncertain. Yvonne got a job first, straight after graduation. She was taken on permanently by the school where she had had a placement. They must have been impressed, though Yvonne was deprecating and attributed her success more to a chronic difficulty to recruit at the school. It wasn't the most attractive or prosperous part of town where the school was located, that was true, and the children could be challenging. I knew too, that the school that offered Yvonne a job frequently took on their college placement students. Several of her colleagues at the school had been at her teaching training college, two from her year-group, including that chap who became headmaster, I think.

I was caught out by how quickly we reached a crossroads in our relationship. We were still living in the different towns where we had studied. I had applied for a few jobs in my university town, without success but now we faced a bit of a quandary. Yvonne wanted me to join her but living together was out of the question for us. Some of our friends had experimented with it at university but their co-habitation had usually been kept secret as far as possible from parents back home. I didn't want to do anything hole-in-the-corner or conduct an elaborate deceit. Yvonne's mother would have cut her off (Or so she threatened) if she lived with a man without the benefit of wedlock. I was very keen to formalise things with Yvonne and was sure I could get something to tide us over in the town where she lived and now worked. With alternative scenarios ruled out, marriage appeared to be the only feasible option at this stage. So that was that really, very easily and neatly concluded. Yvonne's wage would get us a flat, at a reasonable rent, till I could contribute and we could look for a house together.

I am hard-pressed to remember much of the discussion that preceded our decision to get married. I don't recall any formal proposal on my part, the one-knee stuff. It just came to be agreed, a natural progression and outcome from where we were. It had an element of inevitability in the light of our circumstances. That doesn't sound very romantic, I know. But there was romance there. After three or more years together, our feelings for each other were powerful and they had their own impetus, towards only one possible goal. We reached a mutual understanding, at an indefinable point. Sometimes the romance emerges in practicalities, what you do rather than what you say.

When Yvonne and I went back home for a visit and I told my parents that we intended to get married, Mother ran from the room in tears. I don't think they were tears of joy. Did she think I would stay with her always, never marry, remain at home till I was middle-aged and she and Dad elderly? She didn't explain. I can't think it should have come as such a big surprise, our getting married, I had been seeing Yvonne for over three years by then. Dad was happy enough. Shook my hand and gave Yvonne a kiss. Mother came around eventually, up to a point. I can't say that relations between my mother and my wife were ever anything more than distantly polite but there were never rows or cross words. Both made the effort when the occasion demanded it. I think at the bottom they were similar characters, not formed for compromise, so I have to be grateful that they flexed just enough to never create a breach.

It seems very young to be married, looking back but those were the times. These days, living together or cohabiting or whatever it is called now, is almost compulsory as a sort of staging post towards marriage or as a permanent alternative, even after children come along. It always seems a little bizarre to me when you see daughters as bridesmaids at their parents' wedding. Why bother when you have got that far in or if you do, why make a fuss? It is such an expense, an excuse for a big party, I suppose. I don't mind what people do, of course but I can't entirely fathom the thinking behind it all.

By the time Yvonne and I tied the knot, several of our contemporaries were already married. Even, tragically, one of our school friends was already a widow. Her husband dropped dead at work. Brain tumour or something in the brain, not sure we ever knew. She never remarried. One lad I knew at school was married at sixteen. He is still married, to the same woman, as far as I know. Naturally, in those days, there were a fair number of cases where a couple had to get married as if a desperate passion meant they could not do anything but marry, the compulsion of their emotions being so great. The phrase used for these situations didn't suggest the ignorance or carelessness or recklessness or ineptitude that usually brought them to this pass. It didn't evoke the shame-faced conferences between hostile parents, battered by social conformity, to make the hurried arrangements, so it didn't show. It was relatively common amongst our relatives. It wasn't why Yvonne and I got married.

The odd thing was, despite it happening all around us or so our friends and television and films and the newspapers let us know, Yvonne and I never slept together until we were married. There had been a bit of fumbling about (I'll skate over the details) but fumbling is about the right word. I had no idea what I was doing or where the boundaries lay but Yvonne quietly but firmly made it clear in due course. I was respectful and never pushed things too far. In retrospect, it might have been better if we had experimented more. There were, how shall I put it, difficulties, when it came to the honeymoon.

I have been in the garden today. There are distinct signs of spring now. The daffs are out, the snowdrops already dying back. We don't have many spring bulbs out there but what we do have are in bloom and it's a welcome sign of brighter days on the way. I have left the garden all winter, probably you would call this neglect. Even in the dead season, there are jobs to do. I could see them; leaves clumping and rotting, the heads of the roses in need of secateurs, but I ignored them. The lawn is not looking great, with yellow patches where Zeno has peed and some dying areas where the fallen leaves have been left uncleared and the grass is withering underneath. It will bounce back come the summer, I am sure.

I am glad to have the garden. It's an asset for Zeno. She'll happily spend an hour or so each day, sniffing about to see what is new, following a trail where a cat might have got in, chasing off any odd seagull that dares to land in her space. It's well-fenced so I have no concerns for her welfare when she is out there.

On the whole, the garden is what they call these days low maintenance. There is a fair-sized area of lawn, a bit of paving and patio, a couple of small beds for flowers, and a section at the back that runs a touch wild, with a few straggly shrubs and plants. There are frogs in there so I am happy to leave it largely untended; it saves me a job. I will root out any brambles that take hold, bindweed, that sort of thing, but it can be quite attractive at the height of the summer when a few wildflowers spring up. Yvonne always said she liked gardens but not gardening. I am of a similar mind. If I can get away with it, I do the minimum to keep it tidy. There is weeding to do regularly. Most of the offending growth comes from the neighbour's plots, I tend to think, finding its way over or under or through the fencing. None of them seems to be keen gardeners. Some of the weeds are home-grown too, I have to admit.

A significant number of people around here appear to have professionals who come in to see to their gardens. You can tell that this is an area with a large retired population. The local paper is full of adverts for gardening services, domestic help, odd-job men, carers, dog walkers and dog grooming, all those types of businesses that service the peculiar wants and supply the peculiar needs of older folk who need a bit of help and have the money to provide it. There are three chemists on the high street, a mobility scooter place, hairdressers (with pensioner specials), podiatrists, dentists (all private). Every cafe and chip shop does lunchtime offers for the retired. I might get to the stage soon enough when I will happily pay a few quid to someone to take charge of the garden and do my weekly cleaning and ironing. Most pensioners here will have a few bob in the bank so why not spend it to make your life a little easier? For now, I can manage. I prefer not to have too many people coming and going to the house and why make yourself old before your time?

    I have raked up a few leaves, cleared and swept the paths, done some dead-heading and minor pruning. There was a bit of dog-pooh about too, which I have cleaned up. That was Zeno being lazy and me too, likely on those frosty mornings. Just that little effort in the garden this morning has made a difference already. I came inside for a break and a cup of tea, to warm me up. The window cleaner arrived and is up his ladders with his shammy, the old-fashioned way. Zeno is watching him, fascinated, going from window to window as he works, following the progress of his shammy. It's dry today, with a little bit of bleary sunshine but I don't envy those with outside jobs. I had a few weeks of fruit picking after Yvonne and I were first married. It was hard work; too hot when the sun shone and then drenched the next day when it rained. My hands were all callouses and split skin around the nails. Some take to it, I know, many prefer it. It was a necessity in my case. It took me a while to find a job after Yvonne and I were married, longer than we both anticipated. Money was tight and my unemployment did put a strain on our marriage, that you don't need as newlyweds. Yvonne was the main earner, and for certain periods the only earner and she did begin to resent it. There were times when she came home from work, tired and frazzled, to find me bored and hanging about waiting for her. She would give me a look some days, barely said a word, and went straight to the bedroom to change. She could be in there all night sometimes, avoiding me. It did feel a bit unfair. I was doing everything I could to find work.

    I did my best about the home too, keeping it tidy, trying to do my bit but a one-bedroom flat does not need that much attention. I cooked the meals but Yvonne sometimes found fault (I was still learning how to cook proper meals at that point). Friends and family were quick to make odd jibes about me being a kept man (Yvonne's father was particularly free with these comments). Yvonne never defended me. I could see that she was losing patience with me. I was beginning to fear she was regretting our marriage.

It was not a great time nationally, a gloomy outlook, and the town where we lived had suffered more than most in the recession. The economy was turning around but we didn't feel it. My degree did not fit me for any particular career. Looking back, I could have made a better choice of subject to study. For a time at school, I never even thought I would go to university but everyone else seemed to be applying and I thought I would give it a go. Under the pressure of the application deadline, I pretty much made a random choice, never thinking it through or considering where the degree would get me. I had received a good mark for a recent essay in one of my A levels subjects so I picked that subject to study. That good grade turned out to be a bit of a fluke and it was by far my best mark for that subject in all my studies. I got the worst final grade in that subject of all my A level results. But I was already committed and didn't see how I could change my course mid-stream. I did the best I could under the circumstances but it was down to sheer grind that I got through my finals. I had lost most of my enthusiasm for the syllabus within the first term but I battled on, just keeping as my goals that I should come out of this time with a fair to middling degree and that I would not let myself or anyone else down. I did not look beyond finals until I absolutely had to.

After my first job application rejections, Yvonne had suggested I think about teaching but really it didn't feel right for me. I applied for almost anything in the end. I had a couple of temporary, seasonal jobs (Including the fruit-picking), that at least brought in a little money for a while and showed good intent. It wasn't that we were on the breadline or anything. Yvonne's salary was perfectly adequate for us to live on. It was just the blow to my self-esteem that rankled and for Yvonne too, the perception that I couldn't provide for us.

After about a year, I got a job with the local council. It was just an office job really, low-level administration, interestingly enough in the education department. I worried that I might end up treading on Yvonne's toes but it worked out all right, as I never had any professional dealings with Yvonne's school or its staff at any time in my career. I worked in areas related to post-16 education and colleges. I had applied for other jobs with the council, and I usually didn't even get an interview but this time I was lucky and scraped in. It was advertised as temporary, which might suggest that there was less competition for the post, hence my success at the interview. After the year's contract was up, they made it permanent. That felt good. I must have been doing something right. Yvonne was pleased. She still earned more than me but at least I was pulling my weight at last. The extra cash was welcome too. It meant we could have a few little luxuries. Yvonne splashed out on new clothes, largely for school but some for going out. We bought a television set and had our first proper holiday, in a cottage in Wales.

Our honeymoon had only been a weekend away, in a hotel, on a country estate close to our hometown. It hadn't been a roaring success. Yvonne's parents had paid for it as a wedding present. I don't think they paid a lot. Yvonne's father had got a good deal on the package, through his connections. It showed. The hotel had seen better days and we found we were miles from anywhere. That was fine for me but we were thrown on our own company for really the first time and there were adjustments to be made. We couldn't afford to go anywhere or even eat in the restaurant every evening (Only breakfast was included in the price), so we found ourselves snacking on nuts in the bar and making one drink last all night. Not how I would have preferred our life together to start. On the whole, I would have rather that we had skipped it and spent the money on things for the flat.

Our Wales holiday was lovely, the first of our many excursions. We had the cash to enjoy it, eating out every night, trips about the place. I even bought Yvonne a little bracelet, in silver, fitted with opals. It was the one piece that I kept back from Yvonne's sister when she took the jewellery. I had found it after Yvonne died, still in its little box, at the back of one of her drawers. Yvonne didn't wear it often after that first holiday but I hoped she still treasured it. She chose her own jewellery after that first gift from me. Her taste matured, I imagine; she had some stylish pieces, expensive pieces (Some a bit garish too, which I never thought quite suited her).

I put some washing on when I had finished in the garden. This is one of those jobs that I just do as and when required. It makes no sense to wash every Monday when you don't have enough for a full load. It was fine for when there were the two of us, to keep a regular day, now it is just me, I do it when needed. I probably keep the sheets on the bed longer than we did in Yvonne's time. They get changed every fortnight, sometimes more often, sometimes less often but Yvonne insisted on a weekly turnaround. I might wear a shirt for more than one day these days too. If it's only been lightly worn, why not? Sometimes I leave off ironing a shirt, if it doesn't look too creased when it comes off the line or if

I'm going to wear it under a jumper. I don't think this is a compromise too far or the first steps on a slippery slope to personal neglect. I keep to certain standards, I hope. Underwear and socks, of course, I change daily, always did.

I make these little changes to the old regime where they make sense. I like to peg the washing out still if I can. Today was the first time this year that I had put the washing on the line. I could probably have got away with it earlier; a windy day, even without the sun, usually does the trick. But up to press, I have just hung my few bits over a clothes horse and across radiators. It was only this morning, with the weather getting milder and the scent of spring on a gusty breeze, that I took the plunge. It's a grand sight to see the clean sheets and shirts flashing and snapping on a bright windy day. They come in smelling fresh and new and not of that cloying lavender conditioner or softener or whatever it was that Yvonne bought. I stopped using that straightaway along with one or two other cleaning products that still cluttered the cupboard. I think you can manage with just one or two key products. The world, the house, the body smells fine to me, without masking it in the alleged scents of the fruits and flowers of the rainforest. The rainforest will be better off keeping its flora and fauna for itself.

My house cleaning and dusting programme has become a bit haphazard perhaps. Yvonne wouldn't recognise it. Some rooms in the house, never used on a weekly basis even when Yvonne was around, get omitted from the weekly clean these days. The hall and sitting room, particularly in the winter months when Zeno comes in muddy and soaked or the summer months when sand gets everywhere, are always included. I keep up with the kitchen and the bathroom but you can spend half your life trying to maintain standards that no one cares about and only you see. Why would anyone look under a bed or behind a wardrobe, in any case? Yvonne would think I was cutting corners. She would worry about dust and germs and dread what visitors would think. But I see it as being comfortable and relaxed in your own space, not making a rod for your back and not worrying about things that don't matter, in the long run.

Today is one of my gym days and I have just come back from there. My membership is the off-peak type when it is cheaper and less crowded, so it is mainly chaps and a few ladies similar to myself, past middle age, mostly retired, passing a bit of time or hoping to keep the weight down. This suits me. There are sometimes younger men about, pumping iron, posing a bit, in the way that young men do. Sometimes there are men who are a bit older but still clearly dedicated to building muscles or keeping very lean. They are infrequent visitors during my gym times. Not that I feel intimidated by their physique or their dedication to the body beautiful, as some seem to be. It's not a competition for me. Good luck to them, I say but it's not for me, not at this stage in my life anyway. It looks exhausting, keeping it up.

I shower at the gym and sometimes shave too, saving a bit on my bills. The subscription is expensive enough in any case, so why not use all the facilities. It was Yvonne who started me on this gym kick. Apart from walking Zeno, and obviously this only began after we got her, I would go swimming maybe a couple of times a week. I started this long before I retired and I would go on Sunday mornings and before work some weekdays. The pool in Cornubay is more designed for the summer crowd, with splash pools, those corkscrew slides and even waves. I couldn't easily do lengths in there, though there are sessions where an area is cordoned off for ordinary swimming. The times for this don't quite suit me though. Yvonne suggested I join the gym and to show good intent, she would join too.

Yvonne was very slim when I first knew her and she stayed slim for most of our married life. What I didn't know about her when we married was that she was a smoker. I didn't discover this until sometime later. She had taken it up at college she said when the stress of the final exams and assignments got to her. A friend had given her a cigarette and she was hooked. I suspect the habit pre-dated her finals. She hid it from me for many years. You can't entirely disguise the smell but smoking was still common then, the staff room at the school would be full of smokers, half the kids in the playground were likely to be at it behind the bike sheds too. The odd whiff of cigarette smoke on your clothes was not unusual. I never thought anything of it, until one day when a meeting at work finished early and I came home an hour or so before my usual finish time. I let myself in and walked to the back of the house, sensing Yvonne was already home. Through the kitchen window, I saw Yvonne sat on the little bench at the back of the garden, puffing away as if her life depended on it. When the first cigarette had been stubbed out into a plant pot, she lit up another one. I watched with a sort of fascination, seeing this side of Yvonne for the first time. She hadn't seen me watching her and before she looked my way, I went upstairs and pottered about in the bedroom until she came inside.

I didn't confront Yvonne about it straight away, though 'confront' makes it sounds like the beginning of an argument. I raised it in a gentle way. Yvonne, of course, denied it at first or then claimed that it was only very rarely she had one. I could tell from the practised way she dragged deeply on that cigarette that she was habituated to it, so I wasn't having these denials. I didn't like it. I didn't like her having secrets either. I told her so. There was enough evidence even then that smoking was very bad for you and could be fatal. At the time I discovered her habit, Yvonne's own aunt had just suffered a drawn-out death from lung cancer, a heavy smoker all her life. Yvonne vowed to quit and I think she tried very hard to honour that promise. Initially, I suspect her main efforts were dedicated to more scrupulously hiding her habit from me rather than to actually giving it up. It took a while but I never caught her again smoking and I took her at her word when she announced that she was smoke-free. I think she still had the occasional cigarette and I even half expected to find an emergency pack somewhere in a cupboard or a drawer, after her death.

The smoking partly kept her slim in those early days, I imagine. She always missed breakfast and ate sparingly in the evening. She gained a little weight after she gave up smoking; another reason I was inclined to believe her when she told me she had quit for good. That bit of extra weight stayed with her after that but did not spread much, until the time she retired. I think a determination to lose those extra pounds partly motivated the gym membership, though I did tell her that cutting out that glass or two of wine in the evening, and the little more than that at the weekends, would work too. We went together to the gym for a while. Yvonne was often out of breath at even the gentlest exercise and on occasion I found her clutching her chest as if in some pain. I was worried but she told me not to fuss. She did, however, at my urging, go back to her doctor and the doctor expressed some doubts about the gym, with Yvonne's health conditions. The doctor suggested something lighter, taking Zeno out, for instance. She should start with smaller lifestyle changes and build up to more vigorous exercise. Yvonne's attendance at the gym tailed off after this, even for the short sessions on the treadmill she had been doing. She never did take to dog-walking and she still liked her glass of wine. If anything, she said, she preferred to eat less rather than give it up. With nothing much else occupying my days, I still went to the gym, on my own, and I still do.

My routine is fairly undemanding and I have never varied it from the one they gave when I joined. I was never hoping for a six-pack. I am not even entirely sure what that is. I will go on the bike or the treadmill for twenty minutes or so, though it does sometimes strike me as odd that I am paying money to do activities that I could do in the open air for nothing, on a real bike or jogging in the park. I will pick up a few of the lighter weights. I will go on the machines and pull the bars down or push the bars up or press the bars together, whatever is required by the item of equipment. If I'm feeling limber enough, I will get down on the floor and work on my core, as they call it. I generally do about an hour but twenty minutes has sometimes been enough for me. It passes the time and hopefully keeps the blood circulating and the limbs moving. I don't weigh myself regularly and I don't look down very often, when I'm standing in the shower at home, to check if my belly is growing. If I felt the waistband of my trousers pinching, I might step up the exercise or cut out a few calories but it has never come to that. I'm not looking for the strength to run marathons. I'm not looking at miracles, just to keep the motor running. It must be doing some good. I tend to feel better afterwards, if only because it is over and done with, till the next time. I miss it if I skip a session or a week.

In the summer months, once or twice a week, occasionally more often, I will venture into the sea. It's there and I feel I should honour it. Whatever time of year or time of day, it is always cold, the first gasping steps into the water. I try to get that part over with as quickly as possible, not hesitating as I walk in until I am chest-deep. Then I lift off the bottom and start to swim. There's no point going in step by step, it just prolongs the acclimatisation. Get in quick and get moving as soon as possible. Keep your breathing steady and regular, the panting you instinctively start to do just gets you dizzy, I find. You quickly forget the cold, some days it can even feel quite balmy, later in the summer. I love that moment when you kind of bond with the element. The sun is on your face, the shore has receded somewhat, the tide's ebb and flow is buoying you up. Part of the time, I will just float on my back, absorbed in the sky, all thought purged. The whole experience is exhilarating and soothing at the same time.

I prefer not to have an audience when I swim so I will mainly go in the early mornings, as soon as the sun is up when I can have the beach to myself. You don't see that many people actually swimming in the water as a rule. There are countless going in for a paddle, children and adults, kicking and splashing about. Some do venture out a bit further and take a few strokes before heading back, shivering and grabbing for a towel. But I can't say I have noticed many dedicated, regular swimmers about, one or two, none usually when I go.

I am quite a strong swimmer, I think, but I've seen enough of the moods of the sea now not to take any risks. I prefer that my feet can touch the bottom and I tend to swim parallel to the shore, rather than swimming out, away from it. I've noticed those sudden channels of colder water that take you by surprise as the tide is coming in and those areas where the seafloor just falls away and you find yourself in deep, clear water. The odd heavy wave can take you off your feet too and fill your eyes and mouth with salt water even fairly close to the shore. There is a bit of a panic when that happens but I've learnt to ride these out, as a surfer might. These are the unpredictable aspects of the sea, random intimations of its power and otherness. I feel safe enough, though a sliver of seaweed caught around your leg or a glimpse of a flickering fish passing close by, reminds you that you are not native to this domain and it merely tolerates you as an ambiguous guest.

It's best to keep the time you spend in the water short. You only notice that your toes and fingers are numb when you get out and you fumble to get your clothes back on, fasten buttons or tie shoelaces. That clumsy numbness can be a bit scary sometimes. You imagine, what if the cold had crept up your limbs to your torso whilst you were in the water, without you really noticing it. They say drowning can be a peaceful death, once you surrender to it, once you embrace it.

It is Bin Day today. It's an occasion that deserves capital letters, I think. For many retired people, it is the Lodestar of the week, the one fixed point that everything else rotates around. There are obviously things we have to do by certain dates: pay bills, get the MOT done, and order our repeat prescriptions. There are things that happen on certain days in the month (When our pension is paid, is the main one). But most of our life has flexibility and an unstructured pattern that we can't change. We can artificially manipulate it, to make it seem as if we are governed by imperatives and absolutes but it isn't true. We have no work, nothing that needs to be done on or by a certain day (Unless we choose to fix it that way), and nothing that never varies, day to day, week to week. Apart from Bin Day.

I can't recall how many conversations I have had with my neighbours about our bins; is it bin day today, are they changing the bin day for the bank holiday, which colour bin is going out today, even, can I recycle this bottle or is it general rubbish. We get obsessed. We look askance at those folk with jobs who don't put their bin out the night before it is due to be collected (As we do, in case the bin-men come early) but drag it with them to the end of their yard as they dash off to work in the morning. We are affronted by those who leave their bin languishing at the kerb all day, instead of promptly wheeling it back as soon as it is emptied. We make friendly, reciprocal arrangements with sympathetic neighbours when we are on holiday to ensure either that our bin is taken out on the due day when we are absent (Even if it is almost empty) or that it is wheeled back to its home if we leave it out before we go away (Even if this is two or three days early). We scour the street on bin day to make sure that the bin we have put out matches the colour of the bins put out by our neighbours. It would be a catastrophe if we put the wrong bin out. The bin-men wouldn't take it and a month's worth of refuse would accumulate, till it was next due to be unloaded. We test the weight of our bin. We fear that an overweight bin, too full and cumbersome to wheel about easily, must break some health and safety rules and would be left ignominiously behind. We scrupulously adhere to the rules about which items to put in which bin and become familiar with the recycling labels on all the products we buy.

Some people treasure their receptacle so much that they have it cleaned each week, after emptying or line it with giant plastic bags to keep the rubbish secure and contained and ensure the bin itself remains untainted. We write our road and house number on our bins, to deter bin rustlers, to guarantee that we always get our own bin back and help us to spot our bin easily if the bin-men have left it halfway down the road. We have envisaged dire consequences if we end up with the wrong bin. It would not feel right, like picking the wrong child up from school. Some decorate their bins with jaunty stickers or road safety advice.

I am using a bit of exaggeration here perhaps but the kernel of this is true. And I am not immune. I share similar feelings with my retired neighbours in relation to Bin Day. It is a source of anxiety, getting it right, and overwhelming satisfaction when you have your empty bin back in the fold. Yvonne always left it to me. She did not want to get involved. I don't blame her. Bin obsession is a slippery slope, maybe even a sign of encroaching senility; an occupational disease of the retired.

The bin happily emptied and safely deposited at the back of the house, I went for a ramble on the front, taking Zeno with me, though she had already had a walk first thing. The first, pioneering holidaymakers of the year are about, if only in small numbers. Some people seem to like to visit out-of-season; it is cheaper and quieter. I assume they don't mind the changeable weather at this time of year, maybe even relish its occasional drama. There are always day-trippers, throughout the year. Even in the more dismal months, odd coaches filled with tourists still arrive, coming for fish and chips and a view of the sea, before heading off to see a castle or a cathedral. We get weekend visitors all year round, wanting a good blasting, out on the sands, with a dog usually, buffeted by a powerful breeze. Or they brace themselves on the promenade, watching those great crashing waves, with the awe we all feel at that power, dodging the waves breaking across the sea walls and flooding across the prom. It is not until Easter that the first discernible little influx of visitors arrives; brave souls, carrying on as if it is the height of summer, despite it still being a bit chilly, bracing, as we still call it. Children and grown-ups go paddling in the sea, then crowd into the arcades or the cafes that have started to open up, for a warm-up. All that British determination to enjoy yourself in the face of the elements, making the best of it. I admire them, envy them, even.

The kids are the hardiest. When the adults can't face getting their feet wet, the kids just want to paddle, get into their costumes, ending up waist deep and visibly shivering but loving every moment of it. I like to see that. It makes me smile and feel nostalgic but in a good way.

Yvonne never wanted children; she said as much right from the start. She had hinted at this before we were married but once she started teaching, it was clear that her views were firmly fixed. She said she had 30 kids already, her pupils at school. They were more than enough for her. Why would she want more? I could see her point. She gave her life to those children at the school, coaching them, teaching them, keeping them on the straight and narrow. They were demanding, soaking up her time. She came home completely exhausted some evenings, longing for a glass of wine to unwind before she went off to the amateur dramatics or whatever it was that night. I occasionally joined her in a glass but not every night. I didn't really like the taste of it or the effect. But it was a lovely quiet time, early evening, after a bit of supper and I wanted to share it with her.

I was undecided about whether I wanted children. We were complete as a couple without them, I believed and I definitely would not have put pressure on Yvonne or pushed her into doing something that she did not want to do. The burden would have fallen on her, after all. Mother, of course, was disappointed that the grandchildren never came. Not so much, I think, that she was devoted to children or naturally maternal but in our hometown, at that time, everyone had children and, after that, grandchildren and she wanted not to be left out. It irked her, put her at a disadvantage, made her look a bit to be pitied or a bit to be disparaged, not to have the photos to pass round at gatherings of friends or family, not to stroll around the park with the grandkids in tow. She lost face and social standing; she took it as a failing in herself. That was how I saw her attitude, anyway. I felt sorry for her (And she never let the subject drop whenever we visited, driving Yvonne mad). But you can't live your life for your parents, can you?

I suppose I can see now how children can be a comfort as you get older. It doesn't necessarily pan out that way, though. There are plenty around here who don't see their children or grandchildren, very often and certainly don't have an expectation that they will take on the burden of their care if it came to it. Not in all cases. I can't help watching the kids playing in the sea, in the summer, building sandcastles, all the traditional stuff that still goes on at the seaside and not have a few what-if thoughts. It's not something that keeps me awake at night. Yvonne never regretted it and we were very happy just the two of us.

Zeno seems attracted to children. Whilst we were out, she was watching as two boys threw a ball between them, whimpering a bit, pulling at the lead, wanting to join in. She doesn't mind when a small child pats her ineptly or gives her a close hug. She's not exactly enjoying it but seems to understand that a certain indulgence is required with young folk.

We shared an ice cream on the way back home.

The days are getting milder but there are still many cloudy days and sometimes even a hint of frost in the mornings. I think there is something special about all the seasons, something to enjoy, something to cherish. Yvonne did not like the cold. She was not one for pulling on wellies and donning an extra jumper, to enjoy the outdoors. I think if she had just put on a few additional layers she would have fared better but she was not one for looking frumpy. The heating was always turned up high and the curtains closed early in the darker months.

Some years I am reluctant to let winter go, enjoying the crisp mornings and the way it closes in around you at night. Some years when the season is grizzly, damp and foggy, winter can overstay its welcome and I look forward to warmer days. I am probably the last chap in town to go into shorts. It always feels like a definitive moment, and one I have to be sure about, to pull on my shorts and thereby acknowledge and mark the start of summer. I remember that old saying about not casting clouts and it would feel foolish to take this step prematurely and have to retreat back to the comfort of long trousers. Maybe I hesitate also because I was a little self-conscious of my legs in my early life. The transition from short pants to long was a significant rite of passage when I was young. Not now, of course, even toddlers are seen in long pants. When I was growing up, the boy who was still wearing short pants, long after his contemporaries were luxuriating in grown-up trousers, was an oddity. I was a little late, I think. Mother liked to view me as less grown-up than I actually was, still her little boy. The rules too were beginning to relax later in my childhood, that transition not such a moment of ceremony. Perhaps my reluctance to go back into shorts for the summer connects with this childhood experience. Or perhaps I just don't think I have the legs to carry it off, particularly after a long winter, when the pale calves come out, nearly hairless in places now, looking a bit emaciated and vulnerable. This year, I fear it is going to be another few months before I take the plunge. Not that anyone much cares or notices here. Some chaps, particularly the younger ones, stay in shorts all year round. One chap even wears a kilt about town, year-long. No one really bats an eye.

One downside of shorts is pockets. In the colder months, in your overcoat, trousers and cardigan, you are spoilt for a choice of pockets. Walking a dog, you need them. Keys and wallet, you have to carry, hankies maybe. Certainly, I need pockets for treats for Zeno and pooh bags to clean up after her. I also always carry my mobile phone. Not that anyone is likely to need to contact me urgently these days but it is there in case of emergencies. I do worry sometimes, alone on a deserted beach, Zeno off chasing a seabird, the tide turning, surrounded by wet sand and slippery rocks. I worry about twisting an ankle (Or at least I am always conscious of it as a possibility). I worry about tripping over a rock, about the tide creeping up unnoticed and cutting off our retreat to safety. It is good to be aware of these things. No one should take time, tide, and weather for granted or forget that the coast is not wholly a benign place. A mobile phone could get you out of danger. It gives a bit of comfort when a spike of anxiety descends and the natural world seems full of unexpected dangers. I have had the odd scare, when I have almost tumbled, catching my toe on a rock, my eyes focussed on the waves breaking and not on where I was placing my feet. You can feel very alone, all of a sudden.

Of course, it was Yvonne who insisted I have one. I would like to say that this arose from a concern for my welfare, wandering about the beach, sometimes before light or after dark. That she needed the comfort of being able to immediately contact me if I failed to return home, safe and sound, at the expected hour. I think the truth really was that Yvonne liked me to be on hand, at the end of a phone, wherever she was, wherever I was if she needed dropping off somewhere or collecting from one of her regular activities. If her evening class overran or she lost track of time out with a friend or her plans changed at the last minute, at least she could reach me and I would be there, without fail, to bring her home or take her on somewhere. I resisted getting a phone for a long while. I was a little slow, more than a little slow, to accommodate the technological advances of the modern world but in the end, even I could see the practical advantages of having one. Yvonne always hated to disturb me and didn't abuse my availability or take it for granted. She was always very apologetic if she called on me. I was happy to oblige, day or night, in any case.

I don't think the damned thing has rung more than twice in the years since Yvonne passed away. I would be startled if it did nowadays. I am not even sure what the ringtone is. I charge my phone up as a matter of course every couple of days and it stays there in my inside pocket when I am out, a solid block of reassurance. On the few occasions that I have forgotten to take the phone out with me, I can get a momentary panic when I realise it is not there. Generally, then I would put Zeno back on the lead and head back home promptly. It must make Zeno wonder where the fire is, what happened to our walk.

There was one occasion, and thankfully, only one occasion when the phone did come into its own and save the day. We had not been living in Cornubay very long and my walking routine with Zeno was not as fixed as it is now. For whatever reason, I lost Zeno. We were out on the beach; it was quite early and still a bit gloomy. I was walking towards the lighthouse up the coast when I suddenly realised that Zeno was not with me. I looked around, up and down the beach, towards the sea, towards the cliffs, and there was no sign. Naturally, I called for her and retraced my steps. You can imagine I was concerned and as time went on close to the border of panic. By then, I had run all the way back to the point where we had come onto the beach, calling for Zeno all the way. I had then run back up the beach to the point where I had noticed she was not with me. I was becoming exhausted. Finally, I went back down the beach, to gain access to the area above the cliffs, where a number of caravans were housed. I raced around the caravans and still no sign. I met very few people as I searched; those I met, when I asked, had seen no sign of Zeno. Just at the point where I was turning back for home, to see if she had made her way there, my phone rang. My first thought was that it was Yvonne but it was a man's voice I heard. It was a neighbour on the street. He had seen Zeno on our doorstep, pawing at the door, racing around the garden and even running up the street and back to the house. Zeno thankfully had allowed him to approach her. He had held her and read the mobile phone number on her collar. It was an enormous relief when I got the call. I was by then only a few streets away and we were soon reunited, both of us overjoyed to see the other.

To this day, I have no idea what happened. Zeno might have had her attention caught by something on the beach, she might have paused too long, exploring and looking up, found me nowhere in sight. She must have tried to locate me, most likely in completely the wrong direction, racing up and down the beach. Perhaps I had turned that corner on the headland and was out of her vision. In the end, disorientated and panicked, she must have finally resolved to find her way home. I was glad that she already had her local bearings, enough to find her way back. But I was very concerned that she must have crossed at least one road to get to our house. If Yvonne had been home, there would not have been a problem. With a swift bark, Zeno would have alerted her that she was at the door. I was very grateful to my neighbour for catching Zeno. He must have recognised her, though I hardly knew the man.

After this incident, I was always careful to keep Zeno in sight on our walks. I think she did the same with me too, for a while anyway. We were both a little nervous of a distance opening up between us on our walk. It had scared us both and it has never happened again. At least on that occasion, I had thought thank goodness for the mobile phone.

The cafe was busy this morning. Days like this are more usual in the summer season, with queues out of the door. This does not happen too often but sometimes. I've occasionally been disappointed when I have trekked up to the cafe. I can't bear a scrum so I would rather give it a miss when it is thronged with folk. It's hard to predict and it is rare outside the peak summer months but today there seemed to be a great many burly middle-aged men in leathers, and some women too, crowding near the cafe. They hold a biker event, whatever that entails, at a caravan site up the coast around the May bank holiday and there is always a bit of a spill-over down here when it is on. If I expected to get my usual table I was going to be out of luck. This was one of those days when I contemplated altering my routine and just going home for cereal and a cup of tea. As it turned out, several in the queue took up seats outside. It was a relatively warm day; the sun was cutting a sparkling path from the horizon to shore. There were still some free tables inside, so I decided to stay.

I got a small table near the counter. No sea view but I have that every day, so I was not deprived. Despite the queues, my breakfast came promptly and was perfectly cooked. I stirred my tea and watched the comings and goings, the bikers looking hot and uncomfortable in their gear. I had an angle on the little car park and could see the monster bikes, leaning idly in rows out there. They were well-maintained, spotlessly clean, gleaming in the sun. I caught a glimpse of Geoff coming across the car park. He would struggle to find a table now, I thought. He entered and looked around, a bit defeated. He saw me and there was a brief, enquiring look on his face. I am not sure whether I made a small gesture, indicating the empty seat at my table. I may have done. I felt sorry for him. Like me, he seemed to have his regular routines and it can be disconcerting when they are disturbed. He came over and asked me formally if he could join me. I could see no reason to object, in fact, I was glad that he had asked.

Geoff ordered his breakfast at the counter and came back to sit opposite me. He looked a bit flustered, red in the face, hassled. He seemed to have misjudged the weather, thought it might be cooler than it turned out to be, and had worn too many layers. The day had started on the cool side but had become warmer as the sun got up. Clearly, Geoff had built up a bit of a sweat on his way over. He peeled off his thick coat and dabbed at his forehead a bit, looking ever so slightly grumpy.

"Busy, this morning," he said finally, trying to be cheerful.

"Lucky to get a table, I was about to give up on it."

Geoff is a more long-term resident than I am, I think. We have barely exchanged more than pleasantries, so I am not sure why I say that. He just gives that impression like many do round here, who have been here a while. They appear to know more people, say hello to more people when they are out and about, spend longer chatting when they meet. They seem to be better acquainted with the streets and facilities, stride about with greater purpose. They are not making new discoveries or ambling around to see the sights. They know where they are going and what they are going to do when they get there. They always get a greeting by name in the local shops and their orders are anticipated. I am beginning to be known by some, in some places but I don't think I seek it. I don't hang about in shops or the library after I have got what I came for. I'm polite, I hope, friendly to a point but not overly so. Yvonne was the one with the social skills and the inclination to exercise them.

Geoff must be a couple of years younger than me or just better preserved. I think younger. I'm hopeless at describing people. If I was pressed I would say Geoff is of average height and build, balding and grey to the temples; what remains of the hair has a reddish look and is cropped short. I know from that summary, I could be describing anyone in a certain age bracket, including myself. I don't like to observe people close enough to tell their eye colour and such like, seems a bit intrusive. He dresses younger than I do. The short-sleeved shirts he favours in the summer are louder than I would wear; the shorts longer and more patterned. That might be just the legacy of Yvonne. She was the greater influence on my choice of clothes. I think she liked to see me as more mature, more staid, than her in terms of dress, outlook and even in years, though she was actually two months older than me. Maybe keeping me a bit fuddy-duddy made her look fresher and more youthful. I have bought hardly any new clothes since Yvonne's death, apart from socks and underwear, so my style, if you can call it that, is what she left to me. People fuss less about what they wear in a seaside town. You dress for the weather and all sorts are commonplace. No one bothers, as long as you are decently covered, that is.

Whilst I ate and Geoff waited for his breakfast to arrive, he leaned across the table and offered me his hand. "Don't think we've done the formal stuff," he said, "Geoff."

I wiped my hands on my paper napkin and shook his hand. "Paul," I said.

Geoff's food arrived and we both ate. Geoff commented again on the weather and we discussed tide times. Neither of us appears to be the out-going type and maybe we have become too used to our own company to find conversation in this kind of situation easy. We weren't exactly chatty but we also didn't seem to feel awkward.

I had finished my breakfast and was sipping my tea. I noticed Geoff pushing aside the mushrooms on his plate.

"I did tell them, no mushrooms," he said.

"They are busy. Bound to be the odd mistake. I can't stand mushrooms, either," I said, "but they did leave them off my plate. I hate the texture and that grey ooze on your plate."

"Don't. You're putting me off." He was making slow work of his meal.

"I enjoyed my breakfast very much this morning. You do build up an appetite after a walk on the beach, with the dog. Sets you up for the day."

"Still, it's quite warm today," said Geoff, "too warm for me to eat much"– he pushed his plate away – "I think I've finished."

I looked across, there was a good bit left on his plate.

"You should take the bacon and sausage back for Bella."

"Is it good for her?" he asked. "Might be a bit too salty. She has a delicate stomach."

"Well, mind if I take it?"

Geoff shrugged. "Be my guest," he said.

I gathered up the meaty bits in a napkin. Zeno would eat it, definitely.

"Waste not, want not."

I left Geoff finishing his coffee.

"Thanks for letting me share your table," he said, as I stood up to leave, "nice to have a bit of company at breakfast, for a change. I appreciate it."

I walked back home, through the car park, admiring the bikes on my way. Never catch me on one of those.

I am thinking of having a little drive out today. Take Zeno into the country. A good long walk. We have had a few nice days of late, between the cloudy days and the wet days. Summer has not quite broken through yet but I don't think we will have rain today. It is still on the cool side generally for the time of year but the lanes look green and white, frothy with those hedgerow plants, that I can never quite remember the names of. If we waited until it was blazing hot we never would make it out on a jaunt.

I learnt to drive whilst still in the sixth form. My father encouraged it and largely paid for it. "The most useful examination you'll ever take," he said, frequently, with one of his looks. As you might gather from that, he was sceptical about the benefits of further and higher education. He could not see the point of my going to university. Father pointed out that I wasn't an academic high-flyer, so how would I benefit? Why waste three more years, rather than getting stuck into work straight away. He was correct in that I hadn't done brilliantly well at A levels or at any of my other examinations through the years, just chugged along in the middle somewhere. However, I had done well enough to have offers from a couple of universities. I wanted to go. Everyone else was going or said they were hoping to go. I didn't want to miss out on this life-changing or life-enhancing experience. A generation of working-class boys and girls were making their way through university now. Even our school had begun to actively encourage us to have a go.

Mother was supportive. Well, there were precious bragging rights in having a graduate in the family, the first of us ever to go to university. She was proud as punch at the graduation ceremony, with minor royalty handing me my degree. She had bought a hat as if it was Ascot. My father did not come; could not be spared the time off work.

On reflection now, Dad might have been right about university. I missed Yvonne whilst away and maybe that made me a bit cautious about making friends or getting too close to others as if it suggested some kind of disloyalty or even a lack of faithfulness. Nonsense, I realise but I do think something of the sort inhibited me a little from joining in, enjoying myself too much, in case Yvonne found out that I was having a great lark, instead of generally pining for her company. I am not sure if Yvonne looked at it this way. I doubt she did and might even have been surprised at my suggestion that I had this view. It was not a conscious thing at the time, just a vague sense that university was a bit of a hiatus, not to be given too much weight or significance, whilst I waited for my life with Yvonne to resume or even to begin properly.

In terms of any marketplace benefits, I am not sure how career-enhancing my degree was. I imagine, as my father had hinted, that I could have got farther and quicker, if I had gone into employment straight from sixth form or even at sixteen. It's impossible to know but I do know that I don't always identify when contemporaries look back and say that university was the making of them or that those times were the best days of their lives.

Anyway, I was thinking about when I passed my driving test and have rambled away from the point. I passed the first time. It was one skill that seemed to come easily to me. I had very few lessons, as I recall. My father took me out too, and luckily, I did not test his patience too much. It seemed that this was one area that he might have been ever so slightly proud of me. I think the test might have been easier to pass in those days. A scanty knowledge of the Highway Code would get you through; there were fewer cars on the road, a slow-motion three-point turn did not create a tailback, as it might today. I don't recall motorway driving ever even being mentioned in my lessons or in the test and parallel parking was seen as an evolutionarily determined attribute of the average male without having to verify it. Mostly, I think, in those days it was the ignorance and self-confidence of youth that got me through. You never perceived the danger, never saw the difficulty. If Uncle Derek with his memory issues, his bad eyesight and his wobbly legs could certifiably take to the road, then how difficult could it be? It can be dangerous, passing so young but I was a good driver, not a reckless one. I drove safely and when required, cautiously. I have never had a speeding ticket, never been photographed in a bus lane, never even been tempted to pick up a mobile phone at the wheel. I have never been in an accident, even when faced with challenging behaviour from other drivers. Keeping your distance is the key, I think; never get too close that you can't get out of trouble. Maybe that is a life lesson too.

I had half-imagined that passing my test at the first attempt and with minimal investment, might mean Dad would buy me a car. I was mistaken. Money was tighter than I understood. It was never promised beforehand and never mentioned after I passed. I was not crass or selfish enough to bring it up. Mother could have expensive tastes and my father earned less than their lifestyle suggested. There was a bit of over-reaching in social matters. What I felt a little put out by was that my father did not even let me borrow his car when I asked. I think it might have been an issue with the insurance. He was inordinately proud of his vehicle, washed it every weekend, polished it, and did almost daily checks under the bonnet and around the wheels. I keep my car clean, of course, but when it's in the garage for weeks on end, I don't bother about it at all. Dad would take me out from time to time to stop me from getting rusty. He always sat in the passenger seat, strapping up his seatbelt ostentatiously (I had noticed that he didn't always wear it when he drove alone), as if we were going on a racetrack. He rarely commented as we drove, so he must have been comfortable, there might just be a little gripping of the sides of his seat if we were travelling on a faster road. We generally went by train or coach when the family went on holiday. My father was not as confident on roads he was not familiar with. He avoided motorways (I suspect that he never drove on one in his life). I thought it interesting that someone so outgoing and assured in most areas of his life – at work, at home, in a social setting - should be so lacking in confidence in other areas. Another life lesson, I should have taken more notice of.

It was not until I had been working for a couple of years, that Yvonne and I were in a position to buy a car of our own. By then, I had not driven regularly for about six years. Some of my youthful nonchalance behind the wheel had dissipated over that time, in other areas too. I felt a little more cowed by life and more tentative in any endeavour. I considered taking a few refresher lessons or asking my father to take me out in my new car. But I was nervous of additional expense and Dad and Mother had not yet ventured across the Pennines to visit us, for whatever reason, so I didn't think he would come alone to drive around unfamiliar streets. Yvonne was keen to go for a spin, so I went out by myself stealthily in the evenings after work for a week or so to get back in the swing. It was enough. The touch was still there in my fingertips and in my toes. The car was second-hand, a few years old but it still drove well, to my view, and I knew I would be all right again.

Yvonne never learned to drive. Why would she need to? She did have a few lessons at one point but didn't take to it and quickly came to rely on me for transport even to take her to work most of the time, though that meant an early start. After dropping her off, I still had quite a long drive to get to my workplace and ensuring we both arrived on time meant many bleary early mornings. To save time, Yvonne would put her makeup on in the car, squinting into that mirror in the visor. I found the contortions to get lipstick and mascara in place quite fascinating. She was very adroit at it, after a very short time. If Yvonne wanted a lift home, this could mean us getting back home quite late and Yvonne waiting around in the school till I arrived. I couldn't always guarantee leaving work promptly at five. My day wasn't that predictable. She made her own arrangements some of the time, particularly if I had warned her that I might be late. She might catch a bus or go straight on to evening activities from work. Both of us were well used to public transport but Yvonne preferred to be chauffeured around if it was at all practicable; dropped off at and picked up from her engagements. I was happy to do it. As I didn't care to drink, I usually did the driving when we went out together. I drove on holiday, just by default, I suppose. Most men seem to take on that role, certainly, they used to. Mother never learnt to drive. At a certain period, this would have seemed almost against nature, despite women driving buses and ambulances during the war. That was an aberration soon dispensed with in our town, where few families had cars in any case when I was growing up.

Yvonne was not one for walking if she could avoid it, so we would often get the car out for even relatively short journeys, particularly after we retired. I had hoped that the additional time available to us and the steadier pace of our lives would have meant that we could walk to more places. Why look for a house five minutes from the shops, if you get the car out to buy a pint of milk or a bottle of wine? These days, I like to walk. I prefer to walk. I enjoy a walk. It's just easier and better for you. You miss so much driving a car. Yvonne never seemed to bother gazing out of the window when she had the opportunity to, as the passenger, to look at a view or to get the first glimpse of the sea. We sped past so many features and landmarks, driving through country villages when we got here. Now I explore them in a more leisurely fashion, notice things I never knew existed, sit on a bench to drink in an open prospect of farms and churches I may have seen a hundred times at speed or at leisure and still see something new. New colours in the land or sky; a robin in a hedge, a butterfly meandering through a meadow, even cows that gaze at you with steady eyes and sometimes look as if they are contemplating the great issues of life as they ruminate. The sea is the best and most rewarding for that slow appreciation, over time; always an innovation, so many different colours every day, colours I do not even have a name for.

So, on the whole, I don't drive as much as I once did. I will get the car out at least once a month to get a more substantial shop in, for those items you can't get in the local shops. I still like the occasional run out into the countryside, but it's not a utilitarian effort to get from A to B. There is often no specific destination in my mind when I set off. I will park up here and there if something catches my eye. I probably drive a little more slowly, to see a little more, as long as the roads are quiet and it is safe to do so. I will take a road I had maybe overlooked before, as I come across it, just to explore. From time to time, I do get lost or at least have a less assured sense of where I am in the world, in relation to home. But that's an opportunity, I find. I can retrace my route, if I need to or find a new route back to base. I always keep a local map with me, if I find I have travelled beyond the range of the familiar or missed the landmark or point of interest I had intended to be guided by. I suppose I could find out where I am by using my mobile phone. The latest ones do have that facility, I gather. I am not sure if mine does. I have never looked into it. I find that I like driving at night less and less and I will always plan to be back home before dark. If Zeno is not with me, and she usually is, I will keep my journeying shorter. I have never liked leaving her home alone for too long and I do start to miss her.

I suppose a car is still a necessity to me, though I can envisage a time when it won't be. But now I want to use it more creatively, recognise the possibilities it gives me, beyond parking on dark streets, waiting for Yvonne to emerge from buildings that I don't have access to and have no idea what goes on inside, involving people who may not even know that I exist. I can foresee a time when I will give up driving, through infirmity or indifference. There are so many old-timers on the roads round here that you have to be especially vigilant. Erratic adherence to the speed limit, the sudden change of lane with no signal, you see all this. Farm traffic slows you down and I am not one for reckless overtaking. I can see that the roads round here and the drivers on them might defeat me in the end. I hope I will know when I have become that old codger tootling along with little regard for other road users or the speed limit or the exasperated hand gestures from other drivers or even pedestrians.

I think I will need to buy another car before too long. I have had a few problems of late and servicing seems to get more expensive; the new tyres, new exhaust, new this and that, new parts whose function I cannot begin to fathom. Maybe the next one will be my last car and will see me out. The next one, the last one may be, will certainly be smaller. I will still need five doors so that Zeno can easily jump into the back but this time it will be more in keeping with my circumstances. Not a carriage for a lady, just a practical vehicle for me and Zeno, cheap to run and easy to park.

Zeno has got used to travelling by car, over the years but I still don't think she actually looks forward to it. She seems to know when a car ride is in the offing and might hide in her crate initially, despite what might lay ahead, at the end of the journey. The first time she was in a car, as a puppy, she was sick. It is the same, I expect, for most dogs and even quite a few people. That must have been the first time I took her home, from the breeder. Yvonne had come with me to choose a puppy. Through one of Yvonne's friends, we had heard that a farmer, a little way out from us, in the countryside, bred dogs and had a litter for sale. Yvonne wanted to make sure I didn't choose an unsuitable dog. What she meant by that, I wasn't sure, but she tried to explain by setting out the parameters within which the choice must fall. Size was certainly a primary consideration but there were others. Not a small dog, not a large dog. Not a dog that needed too much grooming or was likely to shed too many hairs. Not a dog that barked too much or slavered all over you. Not a dog that had runny eyes, known health problems or a squashed face. Not too much white in the coat. White would show the dirt. A dog that could be easily trained and did not need too much ongoing maintenance. I had no preconceptions, never having owned a dog or paid them too much attention up to that point. A friendly dog was all I had thought about it.

Zeno stood out from the start. It was quite a large litter. Even Yvonne was moved by the sight of these little bundles falling over each other, tumbling about, yapping at each other, scrambling over the mother, who laid there an image of patience, nuzzling them about, eyes on each of them, keeping them out of trouble. A couple of the puppies raised their heads when we came into their space, showing a little curiosity, probably wondering if we were going to feed them. Only Zeno detached herself from the group, tail wagging tentatively and approached us. Yvonne stood a little aloof but I bent down to Zeno (Not Zeno yet) and stroked her. She responded immediately. We seemed to have made our choice or Zeno had made it for us. Yvonne couldn't see any objection to this puppy, so it was agreed.

Zeno stayed with her mother for another couple of weeks and I went on my own to pick her up. Zeno was just as delighted to see me when I went back for her. But she looked rather vulnerable and apprehensive as I picked her up and she realised she was being separated from her siblings. She was so small and defenceless, cupped easily in my hand, against my chest. For my part, it was love from that point onwards. Zeno's mother was nowhere in sight and the number of puppies that were left had already diminished, collected presumably by their new owners. I did hope that the remaining few had found homes. Honestly, at that stage, I would have happily taken them all home with me.

If you haven't had a dog before, nothing can really prepare you for the chaos and mess a new puppy brings into your home life. Those razor-sharp little teeth, that endless and indiscriminate pooping, the destroyed dog beds and the odd cushion, the frantic racing about, getting into every nook and cranny, and then the sudden flop down into sleep, as if a plug had been pulled. It drove Yvonne mad. She couldn't bear the turmoil, the soiling. We confined the mayhem, as much as we could, to one room, the one with the most direct access to the garden. We stripped out as much of the soft furnishings, vulnerable to those dagger teeth, as we could. I kept the closest eye that I was able to on Zeno, whipping her outside at the merest hint of a squat. Cleaning up speedily the mess on the occasions, well most occasions, when I didn't quite get to her in time. I could tell that Yvonne was seriously wondering whether we could send her back but she could see the bond I had formed with Zeno, so never seriously suggested it. Yvonne did not form the same attachment as I did, despite Zeno's best efforts. Zeno was indiscriminate in her affections and would seek to clamber onto Yvonne's lap if she stayed in the room for long enough. When this happened, Yvonne would take Zeno up at arm's length and gently but firmly place her back on the floor.

Zeno was a quick learner, however. A very intelligent dog, I always thought, sensitive and observant. She learned to not pester Yvonne. There were fewer accidents. The puppyhood phase was soon over and Zeno began to calm down. Gradually, the strict regime of Zeno's confinement to one room and the garden was relaxed and she was allowed some limited access, within tightly defined boundaries, to the rest of the house. But Yvonne made it very clear to me that I was to feed and care for Zeno exclusively. I was to be the guarantor of her good behaviour. Zeno seemed to grasp the rules quite swiftly without too much instruction or reinforcement. She did not disgrace herself or me, well not often. We became quite conspiratorial and always enjoyed the guilty pleasures of a little extra freedom when Yvonne was out of the house.

I took Zeno out in the car with me when she was still quite the puppy. I was reluctant to leave her in the house alone, if I went out to do some shopping or to collect Yvonne. This was all probably over-sensitivity on my part. There was no problem with Zeno being left alone she soon settled, once she had understood that I always came back. Yvonne was not too keen on me turning up with Zeno as a backseat passenger. She said it made the car smell of dog.

Bedtime brought its own challenges. Zeno did not have the same internal clock as we did and she could be still active until quite late. She slept when she felt like it and played about the rest of the time. At first, Zeno had whimpered a bit when Yvonne and I went to bed and she was locked in her crate. I think she missed the rough and tumble, that bundled intimacy of her siblings. Yvonne was very clear that Zeno should be left alone downstairs. That this phase had to be got through and Zeno had to learn that we would not always be there with her, to comfort her and cuddle her. To be fair, Yvonne was right and Zeno's grizzling did not last for long and she soon cottoned on to the bedtime schedule.

It took two or three drives before Zeno could settle down peacefully in the back of the car. She is always strapped in, for safety, even now, when it is just the two of us. Sometimes when we take a drive it is as if she is on sentinel duty, sat bolt upright in the middle of the back seat, eyes front, looking out towards the windscreen, through the windscreen, checking the route, checking on my driving, who knows. Usually, she curls up and sleeps through the journey. Oddly, Zeno always seems to know when we are close to our destination, particularly driving home. She will stir and sit up and look around as if she is recognising the surroundings and landmarks. Perhaps it is just a feature of my driving or stance. Perhaps I slow down a little more or my body language changes, as I look about for a parking space or breathe a little easier as we approach the familiar streets of home. As I said, Zeno is intelligent and observant.

Zeno is ready in her harness and collar, looking eager to be off. I have water for her and some kind of fruit juice for me. I have some chicken sandwiches and a bag of crisps for when we stop, that we will share. I have treats and a towel, just in case. I have pooh bags, wallet and mobile phone. We are all set for the road.

It's a Tuesday today so I am looking forward to breakfast at the cafe. I was up early so it's still a little while before I need to take Zeno out for a walk. She is used to my early rising, even my pottering about during the night. It doesn't seem to disturb her. Even if I open the door to her crate, if it is getting towards morning and I have given up on the idea of sleep, she will often just stay in there. She notes that I am about, lifts her head up, gazes about, sees it's still a bit on the dark side, probably still chilly out, and tucks herself back into the warmth of her blankets.

I have always been more of the early bird. Yvonne was more of a night owl. I like the quiet before the world gets going, the stillness outside and the peace of indoors. I like hearing the first bird sing in the morning, as dawn shows its face, the sounds you hear before cars take to the roads, the leaking of light into the sky, such different colours to the fall of evening. Yvonne would have a lie-in whenever she could, the morning always a bit of a rush when she roused herself on a workday. I prefer to ease myself into the day. I could not see how dashing about, grabbing stuff here and there, racing against the clock to be ready and out of the house, prepares you mentally for the rigours of the day.

Whilst Yvonne could stay up till the birds were starting to sing, I have tended to go to bed early, usually by nine o'clock. Certainly, since Yvonne died I have no reason to stay up late. I don't find the television keeps my attention much anymore or not enough to detain me from my bed. I often read for up to an hour before I roll over to sleep. Growing up, I was not a big reader. I can't remember there being many books in the house, apart from the Bible and a two-volume encyclopaedia. Mother had her romances, borrowed weekly from the library in town and Dad had his car manuals and the odd book about the war or about railways. We had books at school and there was reading in class but nothing that inspired a passion in me for it. In the days when I was working, there were sometimes documents to familiarise myself with, that I might take to bed with me, ready for work. I might get a paper at the weekend and keep it going for most of the week.

Yvonne was the one for books but that is not equal to saying that she was the one for reading. There were sometimes books the size of house bricks, sat beside her bed that I don't think she ever opened or got beyond the first few chapters. I think she had good intentions, getting all those prize-winning novels when they came out in paperback, accumulating well-reviewed volumes of history and popular science, building a collection of important literature, but she had to keep ahead of the children, prepare for her lessons, be knowledgeable about the latest professional theories, so reading for pleasure had sometimes to be sacrificed. I think Yvonne must have got rid of quite a bit of her book collection when we moved here.

We joined the library here soon after we arrived. From the start, Yvonne borrowed more books than me. To have something to do whilst she browsed the shelves, I began to look for books on local history, guidebooks and stuff about wildlife and sea-life, in anticipation of days out here, to look well-informed when we visited points of interest or rambled about the countryside. It didn't quite pan out like that but I still developed an interest and a habit of reading before bed. I have graduated to novels. I started with science fiction and detective stories but I have since made some deliberate choices of books that would stretch me a bit, make me think. Not just stuff to help send me off to sleep but books that force me to use my brain. I find that the charity shops in the town can also sometimes yield interesting results, once you find your way around and begin to recognise the covers of romance and the easy reads that make up half the stock. Books that haven't grabbed me after a few pages can go back to the charity shop. Nothing is lost and the good causes get a couple of quid out of it. If a book has drawn me in and does what the blurb often says but rarely delivers, in other words, made it difficult to put down, I will pick it up now and then during the day. Otherwise, I will save my reading for bedtime. I can't say I have bought a book from a bookshop, for many years, though I do think about it every so often, when I find an author I want to follow. I will get round to it but it means a drive out somewhere. There might come a time when I have pretty much exhausted the library and local charity shops, as a source for reading material, if I live long enough. There is the internet. I do know that. Buying books online and so on. I will get round to that stuff at some point.

I can hear Zeno stirring, so it must be getting close to feeding time for her, and her walk shortly afterwards. I'll have a shower first, though, and dress properly.

Geoff and I seem to have inaugurated a new arrangement. Since we first shared a table, we have had breakfast together for several Tuesdays in a row. It is not that we have made any definite arrangement, though we might fix things more formally in due course. We tended in the past to coincide at the cafe, our schedules just running on similar lines, so it naturally came about, without any planning or organising. The Tuesday after the busy day when he first joined me at my table, I saw him come in, look around, hesitate, and then spot me. I think I half rose from my chair, as he approached so that he could see where I had sat. Maybe I had a slight expectation. Perhaps he was just going to say good morning and pass on but there must have been that small gesture again from me that caused him to pause. Geoff didn't say anything that I recall. He stood beside me and raised his eyebrows, cocking his head towards the vacant chair, as if to say, *may I?* I waved vaguely with my hand at the empty seat and there he was, sat opposite me. I let him have the sea view that time, at my usual table. Subsequently, it has seemed only fair to alternate this. When I reflected on it later, I rationalised that it would have come across as a bit rude to ignore him that morning or just acknowledge him in a cursory way, head down and unsociable. We had both seemingly enjoyed having some company the last time so it was only sensible to do it again.

It's just breakfast, after all, one day of the week. We have not set a time to meet but as if we had arranged it, we tend to arrive pretty much at the same time. I look forward to it. It has become part of my routine. We meet again this morning.

I have arrived back from breakfast. As it was such a beautiful day, I detoured a little on my way back, walking a few streets with Geoff as he returned home and then cutting back down to the seafront, enjoying the sun. I knew Zeno would be having a nap, so there was no rush. Today Geoff had arrived a little earlier than me at the cafe. As I approached, I saw him sat at our table, gazing off at the sea, lost in thought. I could see that he had caught the sun a bit. Like me, his hair has receded and the bald spot is a bit vulnerable. I probably have the same bits of peeling red skin. When summer comes in all of a rush, with suddenly hot days and a blazing sun, you can't avoid a bit of burning. If the sun makes a gentle introduction of itself, over a series of mild days or weeks, you build up a tan that keeps you sunburn free all summer. This year, summer has arrived more fully fledged, a bit overdue, a bit hasty to make up for the lost time. As I took my seat, Geoff was rubbing the top of his scalp and a few flakes of skin drifted to the floor. He was feeling tentatively at the back of his collar, easing it away from his neck, where I could see the rawness of sunburn.

The cafe was on the busy side. I think some of the schools have now broken up for the summer, so it is only to be anticipated. Still, it was quite early in the day to be so crammed. Geoff mentioned this. "The sun brings out the crowds. Don't know where they spring from, happens every year."

We talk about what most people might talk about at a breakfast table, certainly what Yvonne and I did, the weather, of course, first and foremost. Today, set fair but with a bit of a breeze off the sea but likely to be very warm. Our walks with our dogs. Bella not too keen on the breeze or the sun. Zeno picking up some discarded fishing bait (Thankfully, not attached to a hook) and swallowing it down before I could get to her. How our breakfast was. Eggs a bit too runny for Geoff's taste (And they have given him mushrooms again). Mine perfectly edible but I got white toast when I asked for brown. These little oversights and mistakes have come to amuse us, charm us even, and don't put us off coming to the cafe. It is what it is, an inexpensive seaside cafe, with a fairly generic menu and the standard of cuisine that goes with that. It's what people coming to the seaside expect to experience. Still, Geoff does have to say that it would be nice if they varied the menu a bit, put on some other options, particularly in the summer, something lighter. I remind him that there are other cafes in the town, that cater for different tastes, even running to avocados, if you are inclined that way. Neither of us suggests we change the venue for our weekly meetups.

We ask about each other's plans for the day or later in the week. Neither of us has anything exciting in prospect but we itemise whatever mundane chores or pastimes are going to occupy us that day and for the week ahead. Geoff has the dentist. I am going to wash the car and watch a bit of cricket on the telly if I don't drop off. It's just something to watch. I don't especially follow the sport.

Geoff is a widower, like me. We established that fact about each other more by assumption than through discussion. We both wear wedding rings yet are always alone. It doesn't require much figuring out, especially here. I don't know when his wife died; we haven't had that conversation yet. I think we are slightly avoiding it, just to keep things light, and to keep the breakfast table a space where we don't have to dwell on anything depressing. It's just bacon and egg, a cup of tea (Or coffee, for Geoff) and a bit of mild conversation. That is fine for me, just what I need. I have enough time during the day when I think about Yvonne and maybe feel a bit sorry for myself. So it's a bit of an escape from that, something to divert me and distract me, focus on something other than my own thoughts. I think Geoff thinks of it like that too but I don't know. I am beginning to see it as a highlight of the week and these days when I see Geoff in the gym or walking with Bella on the beach, we stop to chat for a minute or two. The dogs look to be getting on better too, after being a bit standoffish (Unusual for Zeno).

The last time I caught up with Geoff, walking our dogs on the beach, we walked most of the way together. We did not have a lot to say. We stopped to admire the view at one point. The tide was very low and the sea seemed a distant blur of blue and green, placid and far away. The sun was almost directly overhead and Geoff commented with a smirk that I had finally succumbed and had gone into shorts and sandals. I didn't suggest it and nor did he but I at least was tempted to propose that we should take our morning walk together in future. The dogs have begun to like each other's company, though I think Geoff might believe that Zeno leads Bella astray. Zeno is certainly the more adventurous and curious of the pair.

Today is the anniversary of Yvonne's death. It is three years today. Anniversaries don't always mean that much to me. I even forget my own birthday sometimes. I remember Yvonne every day that passes, so no single date signifies greatly. But I marked it. Every year, this is the one day when I still go to the churchyard and lay a bunch of flowers on Yvonne's stone. It can feel a bit incongruous, visiting at the height of summer, as if a dreary time of year would be better suited for a dreary occasion. It's always lilies that I take. I hope she likes them or liked them, not that that makes any sense. Yvonne did not show much interest in flowers and I don't think she ever expressed a preference about flowers for the house. She would occasionally buy a bunch, something mixed, when we were expecting visitors but not often when it was just us. Daffodils in the spring, sometimes, to brighten the house. I would buy Yvonne roses when the occasion demanded, unimaginative but traditional; Valentine's, birthdays, anniversary. At this time of year, the choice can be bewildering in the florist but the first time I visited her resting place I chose white lilies and I have stuck with that choice from then on. They have a stately look to them, pure, sacred in a way. I prefer white lilies, the coloured type look too exotic and I suppose, too cheerful for a solemn occasion. I feel a bit foolish carrying flowers through town. I carry them kind of upside-down, as chaps seem to do, to not make a spectacle of it.

There is no vase or such like on the stone or near it, so I just laid the flowers across the marker when I went today. I took them out of the cellophane and spread them, to make a bit of a show. I know they will rot away in a couple of days and look a mess. There was a brief shower, whilst I was at the grave and the flowers already looked a bit battered by the time it was time to go. I said a few words but what is there to say really? I could ask her how she is but she's dead, that's all there is to it. I could tell her how I am getting on, say a prayer even (And I do say, God bless, when I go). But I feel somehow bogus talking to myself in a wet graveyard, people passing just over the wall, getting on with their lives, death the last thing on their minds. It makes me sad being there, depresses me. It pushes out any thoughts of happier times; it only makes you think of mildew and rot, a life gone forever and a fading memory.

I don't want any stone or any sort of memorial when I go. They just end up speaking of neglect and decay, unvisited in years, everyone who knew the person under the earth too, all dead and gone. In the churchyard, the gravestones from the century before last are tilting or collapsed, their chiselled words of remembrance blurred and illegible. You try to puzzle out who is buried there, their dates and those verses that are often inscribed on the gravestone. Worst are those infant deaths, multitudes lost half-formed. Does the bigger the stone suggest a greater loss or a greater wealth and a wish to display it? Stone angels with fractured faces, stone urns and Bibles, slowly dissolving away, perhaps more quickly than they might otherwise, in the corrosive salt air round here. Most deaths and burials go unmarked, many unmourned, I suspect. We're all forgotten in the end, some sooner than others. I don't even want to be remembered.

It was very sudden, Yvonne's death; a massive heart attack. I can't say it was totally unexpected. I think there were signs. I think Yvonne knew more than she told me. After her visits to the hospital or the doctor's, always alone, never wanting me there or really telling me what had been said, I began to suspect the worst. She said not to fuss. She was fine. But that last year, there was, what shall I call it, a bit of desperation about her, a grabbing at life, to wring every drop out of it, whilst she could. Did she have a sense that time was running short? Had her doctor told her something that she chose not to share with me? I'll never know. Certainly, Yvonne was out more, always on the go, couldn't bear to be sitting in at home. She was restless and fidgety even watching the television. She drank a little more too. She aged more quickly that year and compensated with a bit too much makeup and dieting. She had changed. There were times when it was just us and we enjoyed doing the things we always enjoyed doing. I suggested a holiday, somewhere abroad for a change, a city break, something memorable and out of our usual frame. She seemed to like the idea at first but didn't really mention it again and changed the subject if I brought it up.

I don't know if it was connected to anything but in the final year or so of her life, Yvonne began to go to church on a fairly regular basis, usually to the Sunday evening service. It came rather out of the blue to me. Neither of us had been regular churchgoers or came from families of regular churchgoers. We were married in church but then most people were in those days unless there were reasons of expediency, cost or, I suppose, principle at play. Yvonne and I went to church around Christmas time occasionally. We both had been to Sunday school as children. Even if your parents weren't strong believers it got the kids out of the house for an hour or so. My parents were nominally Methodist. Yvonne's family were C of E. They attended St Barnabas's, the place where we were married. What the theological differences between the two churches were or are I couldn't begin to say. I know the Methodist place was plainer in style than the Anglican Church we were married in, though I did quite like all the stained glass, the red plush of the things you kneel on and sit on, the candles and vestments. And they had a choir and a booming organ. It gave you a greater sense of awe than the plain benches and unadorned altar of the Methodists. Made you half believe there was something in it, at least whilst you were in there.

Yvonne never asked me to join her when she went to church. I am not even sure which church she went to. I assume it was the Anglican place, St Thomas's. It's the furthest walk away from where we live, though. She might have gone somewhere closer. For a relatively small place, there do seem to be a lot of churches still going strong in Cornubay, so there were plenty to choose from. Older folk do tend to go to church more often than the younger ones which might explain why more churches have survived here. I don't think they all hold the range of services they once did.

Yvonne did not ask me to drive her to the church or to pick her up. I can't say I liked the idea of her walking home alone on some of the darker nights but she might have made friends at the church to walk with. I think she sometimes must have taken a long way home on the way back. The service can't have lasted more than an hour or so but she was out for a good bit longer than that on some occasions. I became quite anxious about it. Looking back, and in the light of what happened to her, I imagine she might have had a lot to think about, a sense of her own mortality. The time away, out of the house, probably alone, must have been an opportunity for reflection. She did seem a little different when she got back, after going to church, perhaps more peaceful, calmer. She didn't talk about it.

Yvonne collapsed on the high street or somewhere near there. I can't remember where she was going or even if she had told me. I didn't drive her there, she didn't ask. It was probably to do a bit of shopping. There were people about thankfully and they helped her and called an ambulance. Someone called me at home from the hospital and I set off immediately. I don't know how long after she had first collapsed this was or how they tracked me down. The paramedics had worked on her at the scene and on the way to the hospital but she never regained consciousness, was unresponsive from the start and was pronounced dead on arrival. I was not given any of the details until I arrived, of course. I must have been told something vague and general, about her having been taken ill. Perhaps they don't want you to panic and be reckless on the drive over to the hospital, by telling you how serious it is. I don't think I did panic. I had no expectation, as soon as I got the call that I would see her alive again. The deep numbness had set in, that stayed with me when I arrived at the hospital and was there for days and weeks afterwards. A doctor took me aside and told me. I can't remember if they asked me if I wanted to see her then. I wouldn't have wanted to if they had asked me but I tend to recollect that they did not suggest that. They offered to call people for me. I assume all this is standard stuff. There was no one. My mind raced on a little about who would need to know and when. I was given tea and a nurse sat with me for a while. It's still a blank in my memory most of that initial period. It stops about there, my recollection. I am home, is what I next remember. I must have driven back, must have had a thousand thoughts in my head as I drove, or perhaps not, just one, Yvonne was gone.

I must admit, I had a drink that night. I made no calls. I let Zeno out. She had been locked in the house for, I imagine, about five hours but she had not soiled anywhere and came to me as I arrived as if I was her first priority, before nature. They know, of course, animals, when death is at work. I made her go out rather than accept her immediate comfort or solicitate. We sat on the sofa then and I had a brandy. There was every sort of alcohol in the house. Yvonne always anticipated the needs of potential callers. Don't think that I ever poured a drink for anyone but her in this house, though, in all that time. It's still there, in the pantry, in murky bottles, on a back shelf. There were a couple of brandies as I sat up that night. I wanted a bit of oblivion, a bit of sleep; it was too much to think about then, all of it. You want it to go away, to not to have to admit it or assimilate it, for it not to be true. If you can keep from acknowledging it, you irrationally believe that you can stop it from being a fact of reality. It's a mighty anticipation of a change that you dread. Of a shift in everything you relied on, that formed the core of your life and being. You can't believe they have gone, won't believe it. You replay the day up to the point of the breach as if you can skip that part and will it not to be there, for things to still be going on as before. That a key will turn in the lock and everything is all right. Nothing has changed.

I suppose, though I wouldn't recommend it as a solution (It just delays the inevitable), the brandy did help me to let it in a little at a time, to contemplate the possibility of a tipped-up world, to get back the phone call, then the hospital, then the drive home alone, and allow a small chink of the reality in, inch by inch.

I slept in the end. Waking I was grateful that Zeno was there, that I still had a connection with something animate and a responsibility outside myself. My first thought was, how do people survive this? People do and must do, every day, every minute probably. But it seemed so enormous a thought to grasp, Yvonne gone. I had to let that alone for a while and begin to do what needed to be done. I found the strength to walk Zeno and see to her needs. It was a relief to have something practical to focus on.

Yvonne and I had never talked about funerals, what we wanted; church, burial, cremation, hymns, anything. My inclination was to keep it local and low-key but then Yvonne had so many friends, a family, and you have to think of their needs too. They would need to mourn and you have to cater for that. There are certain expectations; it's a public event in a way. Yvonne's sister might have suggestions or insights. Yvonne might have even confided in her in a way she could not with me, she might have said how she wanted things or her sister might have her own views that I would be obliged to take account of.

I took all morning to make the call. It was not easy. Yvonne's sister listened but did not say much. I could tell she was weeping and she said she would ring me back later. Then, as I sensed her sister's tears and heard the crack in her voice, I realised that I hadn't cried. Not one drop. I still haven't cried. Not at the funeral. Not at any point. Are some losses too deep for that? Or is it just how you are brought up and conditioned, how you are made? I know everyone cries these days, at almost any minor disappointment. When I grew up, we didn't. Certainly, chaps didn't and women were discreet and unostentatious about it. Grief may be public but not to make a show of it. I now feel that somehow I let Yvonne down by not shedding tears. It was a raw, internal wound, deep, deep inside. It's still only half-healed, I think, but I can't shed tears. One day perhaps, but I also see that you can go past that stage if you don't experience it in the appropriate sequence. The loss becomes part of your life. You find ways around or ways across the gulf. You carry on. Certainly, standing at the stone that marks where Yvonne's last remains are stored, there is no sense that shedding tears will heal anything. What had to be released or expressed has either found its own circuitous way out or it will always be pent up, contained and buried, deeper than those ashes.

I would like to talk to Geoff about this sometime. I haven't talked about it. But I think I would like to talk to him about it. To find out how he experienced it and how he copes with it, compared to me. I think Geoff is a person I would feel comfortable talking to about it. He has been through the same thing but he did not know Yvonne, so there is no personal element. I have a fear that perhaps I let Yvonne down in my response to her death. There is a sense of falling short. I don't know why I feel this but I do wonder, did I do Yvonne proud, did I feel the right things, did I give her what was her due in my mourning, in the scale and the way I grieved? It might be just that old guilt thing, a worry that I didn't always measure up for her or provide what she expected or hoped for in life. Even postmortem, I wonder if I was exemplary in how I handled it. It's complicated to explain. Perhaps I shouldn't mention it to Geoff.

I consider sometimes if I could love again. I look at Zeno and I feel this literally painful sense of love for her. Maybe I have transferred something of my needs to her, as a focus but I could not be without her now. And I wonder what will it be like to lose her? I consider if I had known how it would feel to lose Yvonne, would I have ever let myself fall for her? If I could have had just a glimpse, just a moment of that pain of loss, would I have done it or run away and hid? Nothing compares to that loss, not the death of parents or of friends, however close. It's a chasm compared to those losses. I know I will lose Zeno (I don't think she will outlive me but she might). Could I get another dog, after that loss? Could I go through it again, for those few short years of joy in their company? I know that no dog would replace her. There is an investment of my time and emotions that have been added to make her special. But more than this, it's about could I face that loss again? It's the same with Yvonne. I suppose we all face it (Unless you are the first to go), as a condition of life, the loss of a loved one, 'the' loved one. Could I love again, another person, embark on that journey, scale that mountain, knowing what it feels like to lose them? I think about that a lot and on balance you have to say, yes, I did love and I did lose that loved one but, yes, I would not foreswear love. If it happened again or if I had that time again, would I love, with the knowledge of that potential loss now available to me? Yes, I would love again, now or then. What is the alternative? Some, perhaps, never find it. Lucky ones might find it more than once. But we have to love, we have to surrender to the urge and need inside us. We have to, even though we know the consequences and can see that it brings certain pain. We have to love, because what else is there? If we don't, we miss the best that life has to offer, the most that life has to offer. It is the bargain we make but we must make it.

Having said all that, I don't think I will ever actively search to find someone else. I never understood those people who meet and are married within a month. It took a lifetime to get to know Yvonne. We were almost strangers really, when I think about it, at the point that we embarked on our journey together. The deep bonds of marriage are forged over time. I don't have time on my side. But perhaps I should keep an open mind. I don't believe it happens, not really but maybe one day someone will knock me sideways and I'll never be the same again. Unlikely, I think, at my time of life but no point in closing any door that you don't have to. Life closes enough for you, slams shut a few of them on the way before you even get a glimpse of what lies beyond.

Oddly enough I don't recall Yvonne and me ever talking much about love; people didn't when I was growing up. There was demonstrably love around, not just the romantic type but in families, amongst friends. It didn't have to be spoken about to know it was there. Nowadays the word is everywhere. Whether it correlates to an emotion that I would recognise, in all cases when it is used, I am not sure. It can't really. The word is a bit devalued, over-used maybe. Just something we say. It would have seemed even a bit inappropriate for parents to say it to their children when I was a child. I never said, in so many words, I love you, to Yvonne, nor she to me. I wish I had. We both knew that we were loved by the other but I think saying the words does matter. If I found love again or it found me, I would say those three words, at least once.

Some days I feel my age more than others. Some days you get these general aches and pains. You can't exactly pinpoint where it hurts, everywhere but nowhere specific. The bones are creaking, the joints are stiff, you feel weary, that's the only word for it. Like most people of my age, I have acquired a bathroom cabinet with its fair stock of pills and medication, nothing serious enough to finish you off quickly, just another of those daily signals that you are not what you used to be. For those of us who don't get floored by a single blow, you can see your continuing existence as a kind of slow-motion closing down or withdrawal, the lights in the remotest regions of your life winking off, barely noticeable as they go one by one, until you begin to sense the growing darkness. I don't often think about death itself. I don't have a conscious fear of it. But I do have an active, ongoing fear of other things: illness, loneliness, the removal of choice, of self-determination, the loss of capacity and agency.

I suppose you don't forward-plan as much. Some things you just don't take on. House renovations, maybe world cruises. You don't wake up with the thought, my time is short (Perhaps sometimes you do, after very bad nights) but there is a bit of lethargy about you, not seeing the point in anything, no longer being able to imagine the long-term. Unless you see the immediate, short-term impact on your life, why would you engage with a thing? Voting in general elections, for example, even though some of the candidates are older than you.

Like nothing else, the death of a life partner makes you feel most nearly your own mortality; the shortening of life, the counting off of the remaining days. But there is a perverse comfort in it too. At least you know, at least you no longer fear, the worst that can happen to you. It already has. Nothing compares to it.

I suppose, the way Yvonne went, is the way she would have wanted to go, the way perhaps I would like to go. Something quick, whilst you still have your marbles relatively intact, still active, nothing lingering, in pain, impaired and dependent on others. I am not sure how much patience Yvonne would have had with me as her carer, if she had survived into a sort of half-life or whether I would have had the temperament to cope with it.

Zeno, my girl, has crept onto the sofa beside me whilst I have been musing and I notice I have been stroking her belly. Maybe she sensed I was a bit melancholy. Maybe she felt a bit jealous that earlier I had been contemplating her replacement. Maybe I think too much. I don't take Zeno with me to the graveyard. I would have a bit of a horror of her peeing on a headstone. That is probably a bit of superstition on my part, worrying about disrespecting the dust. It wouldn't bother me and I know that some people walk their dogs there every day. It has started to rain again. The anniversary day of Yvonne's death has begun to look the part but Zeno would appreciate the walk and I could do with breaking my chain of thought so I will get my raincoat out and pick up Zeno's lead.

When I got back from walking Zeno this morning and still in a mood of remembrance after my visit to Yvonne's resting place yesterday, I dragged out from under the bed the boxes where Yvonne kept her scrapbooks and photo albums. Some of these I had not looked at for years, some I realised I had never looked at. I have a photograph of Yvonne on a cabinet in the bedroom, one of our wedding photos on the mantelpiece in the living room and a picture of Yvonne on a table in the hall, near to where I put my keys, wallet and phone when I come in. I like the one in the hall, it shows Yvonne smiling and waving as she gets on a bus. In the early days after she died, I would wave at Yvonne, in the photograph, as I left the house and say hello to it as I came in; just a sentimental thing really, as if she was still in the house somehow when I left and would be there waiting for me on my return. I don't do it so much these days but the photo always makes me smile, smile back at her, caught in that moment.

Generally, I cannot say that I was really one for hanging on to things, keeping mementoes, though my life with Yvonne is an exception to this up to a point. There are times in my life that I would rather not be reminded of. When we cleared out my parents' house after my mother died, my sister and I went through all their old photo albums and papers. Some of the photographs were from years ago, generations of people who were dead before we were born. Our grandparents had all died before my sister, Barbara and I were born. I knew their faces vaguely. Only my mother's mother was at her wedding, looking stern and disapproving, standing a little detached from the wedding party, her clothes dark, and the brim of her hat almost obscuring her eyes. Some of the photos must have been of my grandmother's parents, in Victorian times, a great brood of them, the mother sat at the centre, holding photos of two children, who must have died in early childhood. Where did all these people go? I never knew them or knew of them. I remember having a sense of being detached from my roots as we trawled through those albums and the little envelopes of snaps, the strips of negatives still kept with them. My parents had isolated themselves in a way. We barely knew aunts and uncles and cousins. Met them occasionally at family weddings and later at funerals but they were never really part of our lives. Barbara and I were intrigued by this trove of non-memories. I started to shuffle them into a pile for the bin but Barbara was shocked by this, like we were disposing of a precious archive of family treasures. She was a few years younger than me so it was highly unlikely that she knew any more about the people pictured than I did. I think it was just a sort of false sentimentality. I told her she should have them all if she wanted them. I knew Yvonne wouldn't want me coming home with boxes of old photos, to gather dust in a cupboard somewhere. I kept one or two of them. My parents' wedding photo, a few of me and Barbara as babies and children, my graduation photo and one or two snaps of us all on holiday when we were children, those including animals mainly. Me on a donkey (There are no donkeys in Cornubay); a couple of photos of me with one of those monkeys that street photographers on seaside promenades always seemed to have on long chains in those days, one of Barbara and me feeding sea lions at some park or other. None of the photos had particular associations or memories attached to them for me but they represented a connection with the past, I suppose. Barbara only wanted to throw away the more blurry or over-exposed examples. Cameras were less reliable then, did not do the focusing or framing for you, so could be tricky to use. Everybody of my generation must have a stack of photos of people with their heads cut off or a great thumb in the way of the subject. Any of these type, Barbara was also willing to dispose of. She kept the rest. Must have taken them to Australia with her when she went; maybe still has them. The last time that I heard from Barbara was a Christmas card the year that Yvonne died. The card was just addressed to me. I had told Barbara about Yvonne's passing and she sent a nice letter and a card. I had no expectation she would come to the funeral. Barbara is someone else I am more or less detached from now. We had been close at one time.

These old family snaps I found at the bottom of one of Yvonne's boxes. At least she kept them, though I don't think that I have looked at them since I rescued them from my parents' house, not from that day to this. That family seemed even more distant and disconnected from me, looking at them again after a lapse of decades. But I will keep them. Not all of them.

I was more intrigued by the photos and keepsakes from my time with Yvonne and curious to see what she had preserved, what she valued enough to keep. There were three large boxes; one was mainly photographs, one was full of scrapbooks and letters, one seemed to be old school reports, certificates and some legal-type stuff that she must have thought we needed to hang on to. The birth, death and marriage certificates, old bills and household material, I put to one side, likely to bin most of it. I lingered a little over a small collection of premium bonds, in Yvonne's name, in denominations mainly of ten shillings. The whole stack probably didn't add up to more than three pounds, in today's money. In those days, we all got them for birthdays and Christmas from unimaginative relatives, although I have no idea where mine went. I could be a millionaire and not know it.

Yvonne seemed to have been quite meticulous in preserving and ordering her own memories. The photos were stacked in roughly chronological order; the scrapbooks the same, with labels on them, showing the dates they covered. Yvonne must have catalogued them at some point after the event, as the labels were all of the same type, the handwriting Yvonne's later block capital style. I imagine she felt obliged to develop a more legible hand from years of correcting young children's work; handwriting that was as illegible as most of theirs would hardly do. I recalled that her youthful letters to me were rushed and fluid as if driven by her urgency to communicate with me. There were whole paragraphs I struggled to decipher at the time but I pored over every word. I can't say either of us was particularly effusive in our affections. That wasn't our style or the style of the times. Still, I dreaded anyone else seeing them. They felt so personal. Yvonne was present in them. I have kept every letter that she wrote to me, even some of the little notes she left for me when she left early for work or anticipated being late home. Things of no importance: shopping lists, items to pick up from the dry cleaners or drop off, what to cook for dinner, reminders to empty the washing machine or read the meters, our everyday life. I'm glad I kept them now. It's comforting to know they are around in the house somewhere. Yvonne would have thought me barmy. She told me years ago that she had not kept my letters to her, explaining that she had not trusted her mother or her roommate at college not to nosy around through her drawers. I could understand that, even if I regretted a little that I could never revisit that smitten youth from all those years ago.

So I wasn't expecting to find any letters of mine in those boxes. What did take me aback was that there were letters from other admirers. Not many, maybe half a dozen. It was schoolboy stuff really. Yvonne must have been very young. I assume they dated from before we got together. Adolescent crushes, the odd, anonymous Valentine card. I guess, at that age, a Valentine card or a love letter must have been a big deal. Certainly, none came my way but if they had, I imagine I might have been tempted to preserve them. I did not recognise any of the names on the cards or letters but we had been at different schools up to the age of sixteen so likely they came from that earlier period of her life. Only one was from a later date. It had an address local to her teacher training college. I didn't know the name but I guessed it was a fellow student, perhaps not at the teaching college (Male students were rarer then) but someone on a different course. I couldn't, from this point in time, feel disturbed or upset that someone must have taken an interest in her whilst she was at college. I would have been surprised if no one had. Whether they met or it went further, I could not tell, but probably not very far. There was no follow-up that I could see, in her papers. She stuck by me so I imagine it fizzled out if it ever even began. Odd that she should keep that letter. It was not particularly gushing or romantic, more speculative and tentative in tone, some lonely bloke who perhaps got the wrong idea. She might have been flattered.

I put the letters aside and turned to the scrapbooks. The first few must have been made up by her mother. The usual stuff, I suppose, starting with the announcement of Yvonne's birth in the local paper (I don't think that happens so much now) and a curled lock of auburn hair. This was followed by school prizes, reviews of appearances in school and amateur theatrical performances, her cycling proficiency test certificate, exam results slips, old bus and rail tickets with no context provided. I passed through these pages quickly. The glue had decayed here and there and items slipped about in the books. It did not look as if Yvonne valued this record especially and it showed little sign of ongoing maintenance.

I passed through Yvonne's college years quickly; they only covered a few pages in her scrapbooks. I did wonder then how much Yvonne had enjoyed her time at college. Whether she began to regret her choice of course. Teaching always seemed to be the option they pushed at children who were doing moderately well at school in those days, girls in particular. She never directly said so but I know she found her first placement a jolt to the system and a very stark revelation of the consequences of her choice. Yvonne wasn't one to easily give up on any course of action she had set out on. Always she saw things through but I think she found it hard.

The scrapbooks moved on to our married years. There were occasional clippings from the local press on school events that Yvonne had been involved in; Christmas events, nativity plays, a royal visit even, with Yvonne standing with her children, as they were introduced. She had taken particular care with her appearance that day, I recalled, and she was beaming in the royal presence, proud of her neat and respectful charges. There was a long gap in time between those events and the next entry; a cutting from the paper on the occasion of Yvonne's retirement. Apparently, the article said, Yvonne had been the longest-serving member of staff at the time she retired. The headmaster and the chair of governors were both congratulating her. It was not a great photograph of her; it looked very stilted and staged with all concerned pretending to admire her retirement gifts. Yvonne's face seemed to be averted from the photographer as if she rather resented the intrusion.

Turning the pages of the book, I came across a review from the local newspaper of an amateur production Yvonne had featured in. I suppose it was one of her few leading roles, Amanda in *Private Lives*. The local press never really gave bad reviews. Expectations were low, I imagine, and no reader would have appreciated cruelty or a cutting quip about someone doing their best, without any reward. If someone gave an outstanding performance there was usually a glowing notice but almost everyone in the cast got some favourable comment or other, even if the best that could be said was that they got through the play without crashing into the scenery and had remembered most of their lines. Yvonne's performance was respectfully commented on. She had caught certain brittleness in the character and looked very elegant in the period costume. Yvonne had spoken the dialogue well and clearly had a facility for comedy.

Yvonne had never been comfortable with me being in the audience for any of her performances. She always said she would feel too self-conscious knowing I was there. I generally ignored the prohibition, particularly if she had a chunkier role, and she probably knew that I did. If she was in the background or had a walk-on or was just in the chorus, I wouldn't go but if she had more than a few lines, I would get a ticket for a seat near the back and go along. I didn't want to catch her eye or put her off by being too conspicuous but I felt I had to support her somehow, just by being there.

I think the performance in *Private Lives* must have been the peak of her theatrical career, as it were. Maybe that is why she kept the review from the paper; there were no other reviews in her scrapbook. I have not been a regular theatregoer and don't really have a framework to judge these things but I thought she did well enough in the play. It wasn't exactly Shakespeare but I could still see that it took a certain skill to bring it off successfully. I honestly thought she was the best thing in the play. It seemed well-received by the audience too; there were a couple of curtain calls. Wishing to be well-settled back home before Yvonne got back, I had slipped out before all the applause faded. Yvonne rarely came straight back home from a performance. There was always some sort of social event, usually at a local pub, for the gang after the show. Often I had been long in bed before she got home and she was usually not in the mood or not in a great state, for a detailed post-mortem of how it all went. If I asked, she would mumble something and go straight to sleep. If she wanted to talk about it, she would get around to it in the morning. But the only times she did talk about it in detail were if there had been something of a disaster or a mishap or someone had somehow ruined her performance. Usually, it was some other cast member missing their cue or skipping pages of dialogue (Usually Yvonne's dialogue) or up-staging her in some way. I felt then, and I feel it more so now looking back, that I wished I could have been more than just marginally involved in this aspect of her life. It was clearly important to her. I am sure there must have been ways I could have supported her behind the scenes, even if it was just helping her to learn her lines. I did not want to join the company or anything. Acting was not for me and she was entitled to her own interests separate from me. But I wished she would have at least involved me to the extent of sharing more of what went on, how she felt about it all. I knew that the partners and families of other actors and people involved in the company were enthusiastically encouraged to support productions and half of any audience at any performance were demonstrably linked to someone on stage or in a technical role. Why did Yvonne go out of her way to discourage me from doing the same, I wondered.

 After this performance, I noticed a bit of a falling off in Yvonne's interest in the company. I think she kept it up mainly as a social thing. There were no other big parts and she often complained of how the old guard was hogging the best roles. Even as they aged they were managing to be allocated parts more suitable for someone twenty years younger. I think this is not uncommon in these sorts of small amateur groups. Cliques form, new members are not welcomed or are marginalised, vested interests are fiercely defended. Yvonne had lost some of her influence and status and with it her enthusiasm for the group. It made me feel a little sad for her, even from this remove. Yvonne did join a local amateur troupe when we moved here and had established a foothold. She certainly took full advantage of the social side of it as she had before. But the local group really only did two performances a year: a Christmas pantomime (Not Yvonne's thing) and a summer musical revival, usually one of the old favourites. Yvonne did not have a strong enough voice for solos but she was happy enough in the chorus, usually utilising some bit of business that attracted an audience's attention. Over here, I did not feel the need as much to go to a performance. Yvonne only actually appeared in a couple of productions.

    Leaving the theatrics behind, I turned to the photo albums and wallets of snaps that Yvonne had kept. There were stacks from her babyhood and childhood. It struck me that Yvonne must have been a very loved child, though she often gave the impression that the opposite was the case. Her parents must have cherished her dearly to take and treasure so many photographs from every stage of her childhood and youth. She was a pretty girl, a typical girl of the era; frilly frocks, bows in the hair, pinafore dresses, kittens, ponies, dolls and more than appeared to be her fair share of Christmases and birthdays. Her teenage years did show a bit of a change. There were definitely fewer photographs and fewer smiles. Standing in a grudging way beside her mother (Her father was invariably the photographer) on a crowded beach, arms folded self-consciously across her chest, a scowl more than a smile in evidence. Yvonne was livelier in photographs with her teenage friends. The colours of her clothes were more garish, the makeup more thickly applied as the years went by. The relationship with the camera or the camera operator was more posed and artificial, eyebrows arched, the smile more knowing and teasing. This wasn't quite the Yvonne I knew or thought I knew from the time I came into her life. I only knew her in a school classroom setting at first. There, she came across as quite diligent and quiet, wanting to do well. She had friends in the sixth form, and I knew these people but there were others in the late-teen photographs that were not familiar to me. I had no idea what she got up to out of school. She had clearly maintained friendships from her previous school and maybe these friends were the ones pictured in these later photographs. They were mainly girls in these photos but there were some boys, a little older than her. One lad had an arm around her shoulders. Even at this distance in time, I felt a small pang of jealousy when I saw this.

Of Yvonne's college years, there appeared to be no photographic record. Closing the photo albums from this era was a graduation photograph and finally our wedding photograph, like a full stop closing a chapter.

Most of all I anticipated seeing again the photos from our married life, a period of close to forty years. Like many people, we took so many photographs and yet so infrequently ever looked back through them. I don't think we ever did that together, sitting down and taking out the albums. Every holiday I took rolls and rolls of film with me, to thread into a series of old-fashioned cameras, gradually more technologically advanced but always tricky to use properly and never with guaranteed results. We never had expensive cameras. When they worked, they were great but such a disappointment when the photos came back from developing and half of them were blurred or even just blank. One holiday, no photographic record survived. Not sure what we did wrong. These days, and even during the latter part of my time with Yvonne, it is phone cameras. Even I find myself fumbling for my phone now when I come across a particularly arresting sunrise or spectacular waves or even just when Zeno does something cute. The sea life and wildlife always have me snapping.

During our time, I generally took the photographs. Yvonne was very photogenic, I thought, though she was always a little dissatisfied with the results and she became more and more reluctant to pose for a photograph as time went on. It was because she was ageing. Some beautiful women have no vanity about ageing and that's very refreshing and endearing. Others feel the change terribly, I imagine. As you mature, it is still easy to compose your features and your frame in a mirror to show yourself at the best advantage. When someone takes your picture it shows more how you really are, how you appear to the world. There can be a mismatch. In the end, and even when I thought she was still beautiful and youthful-looking for her age, Yvonne refused to be photographed. She tried not to make a big thing of it. That photo in the newspaper when she retired must have been difficult and that might explain why she turned as much of her face from the camera as she dared. There were occasions, more public occasions like that one when she had to submit to being snapped. But with me, she was insistent and once became very angry indeed when I photographed her unawares, even though it was from behind. I restricted myself to landscapes and picturesque views in our later holidays and excursions. Finally, I just left my camera at home or my phone in my pocket.

Yvonne would from time to time take my picture, more so just after we were first married. In some ways, she was better at it than me, with a steadier hand and a more artistic eye. An early photo, taken in Cornwall, made me look quite handsome (Or so Yvonne said). Tanned and maybe in my best shape after taking up swimming on a regular basis. It was a glorious day too; the light bouncing off the sea was luminous. Sometimes, after I had been photographing Yvonne over and over again in one day, she would good-naturedly take the camera out of my hands and say it was my turn to be immortalised.

My first thought, when I delved into the bundles, was how badly some of the photographs had faded; the colours were washed out and unnatural, almost sepia in tone. The early days of our marriage looked so distant and dated and I suppose, provincial. You see reproductions sometimes from that era on television and there is a sort of glamour and charm about that period. But we both looked like children dressing up. There was a sort of innocence about the photos but the fashions were embarrassing and the poses awkward. There were pictures of Yvonne in our flat, taken unawares or posed to look that way, with Yvonne holding a book open on her lap, pulling at a lock of hair, half her face obscured by a hazy shaft of sunlight. There were outdoor shots in a park in spring, with us both taking turns to sit next to a bed of crocuses. Others were taken after a snowfall, with us both not really dressed for the weather but proudly pointing out a snowman about to collapse. I don't know who took this picture but it was one of the few photos from this time showing us both together. Yvonne was sat alone on the bed in one photograph, inexplicably in black and white. Yvonne's knee was up, showing quite a bit of leg. Was she trying to look sexy? I fear she was. There was one of me in a striped tank top and flares, trying to grow a beard, I think. We were so young.

I had finally scanned through the bulk of the contents of Yvonne's boxes. As I tidied them back into roughly the order I had found them, I noticed a large brown envelope lying at the bottom of the last box. The envelope contained several photos of Yvonne, taken by the looks of them over a period of ten or so years. I wondered why Yvonne had separated these pictures out and if they had some unique significance to her. At first, I couldn't see anything special to them. They were similar to all the other snaps of her; some on a beach, some in a town setting, one or two with a lake and hills as a backdrop. I was about to put them away until something seemed odd to me, I could not recall precisely ever being in any of the places that were pictured. It dawned on me that I did not take any of these photographs. There was nothing too remarkable about them. Only one disturbed me more than most. Yvonne was smiling at the camera, on a more or less deserted beach, her hair was clearly wet and she was wearing a bikini, a garment I had never seen her in or even knew she possessed. Yvonne always wore a one-piece costume if she went bathing (Which was rare, to start with). This was no photograph from her girlhood before she met me; it was certainly the more mature Yvonne I was looking at, possibly around the age of thirty. Where was this place and more importantly, who had taken the photograph? It was very puzzling. The moments captured in this set of photographs must have meant something to her but what was it and why was I not there?

At first, I could not remember any lengthy periods that Yvonne and I had spent apart but then did begin to recall that there were quite a few periods of separation throughout our married life. Yvonne had spent the odd weekend staying with her sister. Once there was a hen party for one of her friends, in a seaside town known for those events that had involved one or two nights away. There had been professional conferences occasionally that she had reluctantly agreed to attend for the school. Then a much simpler explanation occurred, that seemed both to solve the issue of why the photographs had been kept together as a sequence and to shed light on the settings for some of the photos. Yvonne's school regularly held trips for the pupils. The younger ones were given days out, with a vaguely educational purpose, involving museums, stately homes and the like. The older ones had longer excursions or field trips, as they liked to call them at the school. Every couple of years Yvonne was persuaded to accompany the pupils on one of these trips, which involved a few days away, not far, as I recall. The local council had some involvement with a unit near the coast, with dormitories and areas for the study of nature, sea life and so on. I recalled another longer stay in a national park (Which obviously must be the lakes and hills setting). The area where Yvonne's school was located was what was called deprived and this was often the only opportunity that many children had for a holiday or at least the experience of a different environment. I guessed that these photographs were her record of these times away from home, with children from her school. She had kept them together for that reason.

As I packed Yvonne's boxes away, I still felt a niggling sense of unease about the collection in the envelope. My theory about them made sense but why was Yvonne the sole focus of these photographs, sometimes in a fairly tight close-up of her head, with no context or setting visible? I could understand why the children were never pictured. I speculated that this arose from reasons of confidentially or what is now called safeguarding, though this was less of an issue in those times and surely the smiling faces of the children would have meant more to Yvonne as a keepsake. Why was Yvonne always alone, with just the photographer? There were no other staff members visible, and there were no pictures of the location of where the children and staff stayed. Perhaps rolls of film were taken on these occasions and each staff member only received prints of photographs featuring themselves, as a memento of the trip. More general or inclusive photographs were perhaps kept in the school, for display or given to the children or their parents. I suppose my lack of equanimity about these photos was part of my general feeling arising from the whole set of albums and snaps. There were vast areas of Yvonne's life that I was not part of, that perhaps I was excluded from and acquiesced or even colluded in that exclusion. All relationships probably have an element of this but I reproached myself mostly for allowing these proscribed areas to develop, expand and become entrenched, for not taking enough notice of Yvonne, for too frequently not engaging with what was the greater part of her life, for not asking questions, for my silence, for my complicity.

At the moment, I cannot settle. Geoff missed our breakfast meeting this week. It was an odd feeling, sitting there on my own in the cafe. I usually wait for Geoff to arrive before I order but as the minutes passed beyond our regular meeting time, I began to feel self-conscious and got myself a cup of tea. I sat stirring it for a while, letting it get stewed and cold. I found myself watching the door, glancing out of the window, checking my watch, for all the world like a schoolboy, looking like he had been stood up on a first date. I was conscious by this point that the arrangement that Geoff and I have is an informal one. We have never agreed on a time to meet as such and the situation I was facing might well be the consequence of keeping things so unstructured.

After twenty minutes, it was becoming obvious to me that Geoff was not coming but I still sat on, a sentinel. I was in no mood for eating by then but I did get another drink, a coffee for a change, and this time, I did drink it whilst it was still hot. This passed another ten or fifteen minutes and beginning to feel a bit ridiculous, I decided to go. By this time, I was sure that the regulars, that the waitress even, were aware of my predicament and I did not want to be an object of attention or speculation. Why I would feel suddenly exposed, left on my own, when I had eaten there alone for the past three years, I couldn't tell. I got up, as casually as I could, and set off for home.

I suppose, walking back I did recollect that I had not seen Geoff and Bella about since the end of the previous week. He hadn't been at the gym either, that I remembered. It seemed most likely therefore that one or the other of them was not well. At home, I was still agitated and concerned. I was worried about Geoff. Unexpectedly, I was reminded of Yvonne and those frantic feelings I had around the time she was taken ill in town and taken to the hospital. Yvonne had of course been on my mind for a while and I think the Geoff thing just tapped into my heightened sensitivities at this time. Living on your own and with few social contacts, just shows how quickly you come to be connected to another person, dependent on them in a way. They become part of the fabric of your life. It's a shock and it's unsettling when they suddenly disappear, without explanation. It seems over-dramatic but it showed me how easily little things can have a disproportionate impact on your wellbeing when your life runs in a narrow groove. For quite a while that Tuesday, I was very fretful and uncomfortable, my thoughts running down all sorts of daft pathways. Zeno noticed and it made me think again about how much of my happiness depended on her too, about how my life was anchored to such fragile pegs. It was difficult for a while. Of course, I calmed down in the end. Found my compass points and tacked back to a sort of equilibrium.

After another somewhat anxious night, the mystery is solved. I caught up with Geoff this morning, walking Bella on the beach. He looked pale and peaky. He had lost that glow that the summer had given him. Geoff explained that he had been ill, something to do with the stomach. I had gathered from our acquaintance already that both he and Bella were delicate in that area and in other areas. Often when we met, one or the other of them seemed to be ailing in some way, whether it was Geoff's hay fever or dyspepsia or Bella's food intolerances Geoff believed that he had eaten something that had disagreed with him. It had laid him low for several days. I was very relieved to see him, even in his slightly hollowed-out state. I am not one for spontaneous hugs, that's not my way but I did briefly put a hand on Geoff's shoulder. Some minimal physical contact seemed in order. I must have beamed at him as he did at me. Even Bella and Zeno were enthusiastically wagging their tails and reconnecting through scent, in their time-honoured way.

"Why didn't you let me know?" I asked, once Geoff had explained.

I already knew the answer. Geoff and I had not exchanged mobile phone numbers. We had not given each other our addresses. Although we lived only streets apart, in a small town, we had no way of contacting each other. I realised, with perhaps a minor pang of unease that our whole acquaintance depended completely on chance encounters. Without some action on our part, we could conceivably wander through the town for years without ever meeting again. Geoff's absence had made it clear that this situation was unsatisfactory and we rectified it there and then, swapping numbers and details. My first thought was to find a pen and a piece of paper but Geoff already his phone in his hand. I recited to Geoff my details and he punched them into his phone. When it was my turn to reciprocate, I found myself totally at a loss as to how to capture Geoff's number and address. He laughed at my fumbling and took the phone from me.

"Almost an antique," he said, typing away, "there. All done."

Geoff briefly rang my number to show me that we were connected. It made me jump. I felt better after all this was concluded. Would Geoff ring me sometimes, now that he had my number, I wondered. I reflected that I didn't recall ever in my life having a proper conversation on a mobile phone. Many people, if not most people, maintain their friendships and social life in this way, from what I have heard.

Geoff and I walked along a little way, in company, though Zeno and I were at the end of our walk and Geoff and Bella were just setting out. I suggested a coffee but Geoff said his stomach was still a bit unreliable and it might be best to avoid the cafe. He wasn't going to stay out long in any case, at this stage. Breakfast on the following Tuesday, might also best be deferred. Fried food was an irritant. This was disappointing but understandable. To make up for this deferment, Geoff surprised me by suggesting that, after a few more days' recovery, say the following Friday, why didn't I come round to his place, now I knew his address and he would cook for me. I readily agreed. I can't remember the last time I ate anywhere but at my own kitchen table or at the cafe. It would be a very welcome change.

"Shall I bring Zeno?" I asked.

"Best not," he said, "not this time. Bella can be a bit territorial. She's out of the habit of company."

We agreed on a time.

I am up early this morning, could not really sleep. Last night was my evening for dinner round at Geoff's house and maybe I was a bit over-stimulated by an evening of company and conversation. Not to mention a little more wine than I am accustomed to.

Geoff has a little terraced house, close to the centre of town. I knew the street. It was sometimes quicker to cut down that way back from town if I had heavy bags. They are all well-kept houses; just two bedrooms, I think, small front yard and a little garden at the back. I am guessing they were built in the '50s. After the war, there was a bit of a building spree around here. The seaside holiday had begun to take off at that stage and people began to retire here. Our house must have been built about the same time, though we have a garage and a larger garden at the rear.

I had wondered what to take, when I went round to Geoff's, if anything. Yvonne and I were not big socialisers as a couple so I had no past experience to inform my preparations. Flowers didn't seem appropriate, not the right associations, I thought. Chocolates would be worse. I know very little about wine but this seemed the best option, so going largely by price and because the contents had a nice golden colour, I arrived with a bottle.

Geoff greeted me at the door and looked at the bottle I handed to him with a slightly quizzical look.

"Dessert wine," he said, "very unusual. We'll save it for afters."

I felt a fool.

The decor inside was a bit more modern than our taste ran to. It was all very jaunty, very clean, with sharp edges and lines. It was mainly decorated in white but with some feature walls in very bold colours, generally reflecting a coastal palette, perhaps at sunset. Seashells lined the windowsills, relics of the ocean, some so large and ornate that they were obviously not native to our local beach. There were nautical prints on the walls. One, of a giant squid attacking an old-style sail ship, particularly caught my eye. The kitchen looked vast and professional. Some of the furniture gave the impression that it had been designed more for appearance than for comfort. Geoff had knocked through so you could see the garden as soon as you entered. More patio than grass, with borders featuring what I thought was bamboo and those shrubs that everyone seems to plant in a seaside garden. I'm not sure what they are called but I don't much care for them. They grow quite tall. I think they are semi-tropical so don't always thrive here and can look brown and shabby. The leaves rattle in the wind. The overall effect didn't look very dog friendly to me.

Bella was nowhere in evidence.

"She's having a kip upstairs," Geoff explained. I could smell cooking. I hoped it wasn't going to be too spicy for me.

Geoff looked like he was more or less back to his old self and we didn't dwell on his indisposition. He gave me a quick tour of the house before we ate and he highlighted some of the renovations that had been made to the house after it was purchased. It wasn't really a topic I had taken much interest in to date but I asked a few polite questions. Apparently, the lady who had sold the house to them had lived in the house since the early sixties. She was entering sheltered accommodation but had clearly loved the house. Some of the decoration and facilities had not been updated since that time and the house had required a great deal of work.

"Are you OK to eat fairly soon?" asked Geoff. "It's ready sooner than I planned."

We sat at the table. Geoff opened a bottle of wine and poured us each a glass (Something red and a bit acid, for me). The food was pleasant enough. As I suspected, the main course was some sort of curry but not too hot. I'm not really sure if it had meat in it. I could only taste spice and texture, so it could have been anything really. The afters were more traditional, an apple crumble but even that was spicy, Christmassy but enjoyable, not too sweet. There was no cream or custard with it. I think he topped it with yoghurt or something similar, slightly sour. To go with it, Geoff opened the wine I had brought. It was pretty disgusting, very cloying. I only managed a sip.

Bella eventually appeared. Though she looked up appealingly, Geoff did not let her have any leftovers. Possibly he didn't think the spice would go down well but I suspect he is far more disciplined in regard to titbits from the table than I am. It might have been because he had company. Zeno practically sits at the table with me, these days, so I can hardly judge. I asked Geoff about how he came to own Bella. He explained that she was a rescue dog and he had acquired her about three years before. I could see how he might want a dog for company living on his own. They are a comfort. Geoff did not know Bella's age or breed, if she had a breed; most likely a bit of a cross but who knew what was in the mix. She has a bit of a shaggy coat, needs quite a lot of grooming, greyish in colour. She is on the small side, slightly smaller than Zeno, and has quite long ears but a short tail. It might have been docked a little. Appealing in her way but I wouldn't have chosen her if I am honest. She looks like the kind of dog that expects to be pampered. Bella must be around the same age as Zeno, though I couldn't be sure.

"Bella had been with an old lady before me," explained Geoff, "she had her from a puppy but died suddenly and there was no one who wanted to take Bella on. I was clear that I wanted a rescue dog but worried about temperament. Some rescue dogs come with terrible histories, abuse, neglect and so on. I didn't think I could handle a problem dog. But Bella turned out fine. Likes her home comforts a little too much. But don't we all tend to spoil them, a little." Bella dutifully rolled onto her back and Geoff indulged her with a belly rub.

I offered to help with the washing up but Geoff waved my offer away, saying it would keep till morning. I did wonder at that point whether Geoff employed a cleaner. The house was quite immaculate. It wouldn't have surprised me. After coffee, we sat in the lounge area, he on the couch, me in an armchair. I found the chair more comfortable than the sofa.

In the end, as we always do, we that are left behind I suppose, I finally asked Geoff the question that inevitably arises at some point in our circumstances. The anniversary of Yvonne's death was still relatively fresh in my mind, I suppose, so the subject was in my thoughts. I had mentioned the anniversary to Geoff and this lead me to ask him about his wife.

"When did she pass away?" I asked him.

"He," Geoff had said.

"He, what?" I said, thinking that I had misheard or that Geoff was still talking about the parish elections or who had won the bowls tournament, topics we had been discussing earlier that morning.

"It's 'he', not 'she', who passed away. My partner was a man."

That was clear enough.

Did it throw me, that Geoff was, apparently, 'gay'? Yes, a little. I had no clue. The last thing I expected. Should it have thrown me? Probably not, in this day and age. But it was a bit outside my experience. It was a surprise, I have to admit, out of the blue. But did it bother me especially? I hope I can say that I don't think so. I reacted, I suppose, based on what I knew, my life experiences, conditioned a little, I expect, by what was offered to me growing up, on telly, in films; part of life but not part of my life. I know that a lot of what was there, in the media, in the past, was caricature and parody (Even from the supposedly 'gay' people themselves). I hoped that I had evolved from those early impressions, developed a greater degree of awareness and maturity in my outlook. I hoped that I had formed a more tolerant and expansive view of things by the time I went into that small moment of understanding when Geoff said those few words and it became clear to me who he was.

The universities, back when I was there, were supposed to be more open and accepting or as they say now, inclusive. There were 'gay societies' with stands amongst the others at freshers' week; I saw them, heard them even, with discos music blaring, *Gay News* for sale. Hearing that music, I had half expected perfume and made-up types, in the Quentin Crisp mode. I stayed well clear but ended up passing along by them in the end (Maybe I was a little curious, after all) and couldn't help but see that it was just young men generally, maybe a bit flamboyant in some cases. Seeing those chaps I realised you could pass most of them in halls and never know. So, at that moment, hearing Geoff's revelation, weighing everything, past and present, I hope I reacted as I felt my best self should. I hope I conveyed in my reaction or better still, in my non-reaction, that I recognised that Geoff's condition was not unnatural and well within the order of things. That I responded just as I might if Geoff had said that he had webbed feet or three nipples. Surprising but nothing to approve or disapprove of, just facts of nature. It is not my place to judge, one way or the other.

As I say, before university and even after my superficial encounters there, I had hardly ever even thought about homosexuality and had no settled views about it, certainly no strong negative view or a view, either way. Yvonne had a couple of gay friends from the amateur dramatics group. I only met them once or twice, though she had coffee with them sometimes. We met Fraser once, out shopping. He kissed my wife in that theatrical way that I had grown used to. She put her hand on his slim waist and he put both his hands close to her face. It was fine. In the course of their chatter, Fraser suggested that I should join the group, maybe not to act or take part in a production but an extra pair of shoulders was always useful for shifting scenery. Yvonne quickly intervened and made it clear that this was not my thing. I had offered many times to help out, fund-raising, selling programmes if she wanted but Yvonne clearly felt that this was her special domain and I would be out of place. I could see her point.

Was I a bit naive, then, with Geoff? Were there signals I should have picked up on? Geoff was just an ordinary chap like me, as far as I could see, nothing different about him, nothing effeminate or flouncy. Perhaps I had formed my initial opinions about homosexuality from the telly, where it was a bit of camp relief or those darker films where the gay characters were a bit shady or a bit sad, and never ended well. I am not stupid and could see that this was largely an exaggeration for comic or dramatic effect. But I had never knowingly been in the company of homosexuals to see the reality, until Fraser, and he did come across a bit camp.

I may have been looking at Geoff at that moment, to assess whether he looked 'gay', whatever I thought that meant. He was not especially masculine (But then neither am I, if you boil it down to stereotypes). There were no give-away mannerisms or poses. Perhaps I was looking for the wrong things. Reflecting, I suppose, on what Geoff had said to me, I then remembered something that had happened once at the gym. I had seen Geoff doing his usual routine and we happened to coincide in the showers. We said hello but not much else. It can feel a bit awkward making conversation in that situation, like when someone strikes up a conversation standing at the urinal. Some chaps will chat away in the changing room or the shower, no shame or inhibitions, free and easy. They seem to have no qualms about being naked as if you were meeting down the pub. Some are more reserved, maybe covering up a bit, hanging on to their towel for as long as they can, talking to you over their shoulder, if they speak at all, out of a kind of embarrassment, showing you their backside only. I am not unduly concerned these days. I join whoever is there, naked without thinking, like at school. We are all the same really, holes in the same places, fat accumulated in the same areas. The older you get, the less you care, I think.

On that occasion, Geoff said to me, "You are in pretty good shape."

It's not something I have made an effort at, keeping fit. Even at the gym, my workout is a bit sedate and undemanding. I watch my weight, never gained those pounds that some chaps do in middle age, always walk to places when I can. No one has ever passed remarks on my physique, as it were, before not even Yvonne. I have hardly noticed, let alone commented on, the shape of anyone else. You can't help but be aware of those more at the extremes, very over-weight, very skinny, very hairy, very muscular but it's only a passing notice, nothing to dwell on. And I applaud anyone, whatever their condition, who tries to get fitter.

I had no reply to Geoff's compliment at the time, if that was what it was, other than mumbled thanks, and thought nothing more of it. I certainly didn't think Geoff's comment was any sort of sexual overture and I still don't or a way of telling me he thought I was attractive. Outside of Yvonne, I don't have a recollection of noticing anyone, male or female, at any time, giving me the eye or any other signal of interest in me in that way. Maybe I'm not attuned to these things, oblivious. I tend rather to think that there's nothing that special about me, to set hearts aflutter. I do recall once, at a works do, everyone a bit tipsy, someone telling me that a certain person who worked closely with me fancied me. I couldn't believe it and had no idea. It may have been someone just stirring things up or maybe making fun of me. I couldn't for a moment grasp what the person telling me about my admirer was on about, had no idea what the signs were of this interest and had noticed nothing myself. I gave the matter no further thought or consideration. It did not affect my working relationship with the person concerned.

I suppose that Geoff's admission at his house had made me look back for any earlier signals of his inclinations, hence my recollection of the exchange at the gym. Perhaps 'admission' is the wrong word like it was some kind of confession on Geoff's part. It wasn't expressed that way at all. It was just said casually. Perhaps he thought I already had an idea; just a slip of the tongue on my part, an expression of an ingrained assumption to use the wrong pronoun when I asked about his partner's passing. His reply was no more than a minor point of clarification in a relaxed exchange of information. People of my generation always refer to doctors as 'he' and nurses as 'she'. Not the done thing now and not borne out by current experience. It was a species of this kind of lazy categorisation based on an out-of-date perspective that Geoff was mildly correcting.

There was a bit of silence from Geoff when he seemed to be remembering his partner rather than evaluating a bombshell he had dropped. Then he continued, answering my question but he was looking slightly off to one side as if he had caught a fading glimpse of something or someone, receding.

"It's been eight years," he said, "Jim. His name was Jim, my partner. He was a few years older than me but still, he went too soon. It was cancer; his lungs. And it was very quick."

I nodded, as you do. "Sorry to hear that."

"He went from that sticky cough that he always had, to diagnosis, to dead within the month. I hadn't noticed the cough getting worse and he never complained of anything, pain or anything else. I don't think there was any pain. When I tried to look back and see if there were any signs that I should have picked up on, all I could remember was that he had looked tired and I think he had complained of feeling tired. There must have been something, though, that he felt because he got himself off to the doctor and it was straight to the hospital for tests; a lifelong smoker, unfortunately, started at fourteen. I never understood how someone as clever as him, a scientist, too, was so stupid about something like that. He never tried to give up. I begged him to often. He wouldn't even consider it. In the end, Jim said we had to make a truce. I had to stop nagging him or we were going to have problems. I didn't want to lose him and so I agreed that if my expressing concern about his smoking was such an issue for him, I would just let it lie. He knew how I felt about it."

Geoff now looked at me directly. "I lost him anyway," he said.

I could see that Geoff still felt the pain of the loss of his life partner. His eyes had reddened. He didn't cry. Not that he thought it inappropriate or embarrassing to cry, I guessed. But perhaps he felt that at some point enough tears have been shed and you have to let some of the emotion go or it will drag you down. I felt in solidarity with him then. It seemed only human to reach across and squeeze his forearm, to make contact, in grief. He smiled at the gesture and gave a little sigh. I was glad that his display of sadness did not reach for the histrionic. I'm not used to displays of large emotions. And perhaps, even though we shared a common feeling, I suppose I have to admit that I did find it a little odd, a little uncomfortable, to hear Geoff speaking in this way of an enduring love for a man, as something completely normal. Love is love, I suppose.

"Do you get lonely?" I asked him.

"Yes, I have been. I have a multitude of things to keep me busy but yes, I have missed him. I have felt lonely."

I agreed.

After a little silence, each with our own thoughts, we talked on. Naturally, Geoff asked me about Yvonne's passing. I told him the outlines of how she went and how it impacted me. Although I had felt it would be good to talk to Geoff about my loss, and of his loss, I was hesitant to get into a detailed discussion at this stage for some reason. It felt that there would be time enough to come back to this, not delve into it and pass over it at one sitting as if the topic was finished with and need not be mentioned again. It felt too important for that. Plus, I had a certain weariness about it all of a sudden. With the anniversary of Yvonne's death and all my thoughts dwelling on this for so long, I was beginning to feel that I didn't want to go through it again, to unwrap it all again.

Over the period since Yvonne's death, I have talked to several people who have lost their loved ones, whether it be spouses or parents or friends. No one has ever spoken to me about the loss of a child. That is a category of devastation I cannot begin to imagine. After a while, in the course of these conversations over the years, the bereavement dialogue can become to feel a bit familiar and almost routine. It always brings it back, however. We all have our variation; very sudden, peacefully at home surrounded by family, after a long illness, a fighter to the end. The event itself has these obituary phrases we fall back on and use to deflect too much detail, sometimes. Some people want to keep talking about it, others try to forget the last struggle, diminish that memory of the one who goes battling to the last breath or the one who seemed to hasten it on, turning their face to the wall, wishing the relatives would leave them to meet death alone as quickly as possible. These days, from conversations I have had, I gather that drugs often blur those last moments. The dying are lowered into a bath of sleep and morphine and it's hard to spot the moment of passing. Yvonne went quickly. I wasn't there.

My evening with Geoff petered out a bit following this discussion of our losses. I suppose after speaking of bereavement there isn't anywhere else to go conversationally, without it seeming trivial and trite, even a bit disrespectful to the departed. I thanked him for hosting and said that it had been a welcome change. Feeling in want of any other gesture, I shook his hand as I was leaving, said I hoped we might do it again sometime and that I would see him on Tuesday, for breakfast.

I walked briskly back home, thinking I had left Zeno on her own for long enough.

Zeno and I took a long walk today. It's a Tuesday, and I took Zeno out early so that I could meet Geoff at the cafe. We passed the early crew outside the corner shop, waiting for it to open to buy the morning's essentials. Zeno got a bit of fuss and figured in the general chat, as we passed.

"I miss a dog," one said.

"I know," said another, "we always had dogs."

When we got to the promenade, I could see that the tide was high so we could not get on the beach. I always struggle a bit to judge how far we should go or how long we should be out when we can't access the beach. I prefer not to let Zeno off the lead if we walk down the front or cut across town. For one thing, there are signs up to say that dogs must be on leashes, though plenty of folk ignore them, just as they ignore the signs that ban dogs from the main holiday-makers beach during the height of the season. Just as some people ignore the injunctions to clean up after your dog. I have always rather too assiduously read and followed signs and notices. I cannot even pass a planning notice, wrapped around a lamppost or a blue plaque stuck on the wall of some anonymous semi, without pausing to read. It annoys Zeno sometimes when we stop randomly to peruse a notice board or similar, and she might tug impatiently at first before settling. Of course, she doesn't mind the halts at certain lampposts, where many dogs have gone before.

I know when we have been walking on the beach that Zeno will have got enough exercise to satisfy her needs and sufficient sensory and olfactory stimulation from all the scents and sights left by the tide and other beach visitors. Off the lead, she will have her little runs across the sands and her regular pauses at every dead fish or dismembered crab or stranded flotsam. On the lead, away from the beach, her pace and her route are determined by me and I am not always sure she has had enough until I see her begin to flag. Today, I went a bit too far and we sat on a bench on the return journey home to get our breath back. As we sat, a chap I have seen around ambled up to us, a bit unsteadily and sat beside us.

Zeno sniffed him and found the odour a little richer and more entertaining than I did. He petted her and she seemed to like it, though she does not take to everyone.

"Nice dog," he said, to her or to me, I wasn't sure; neither of us responded. He had found a spot behind Zeno's ear and she seemed to be enjoying the attention. "I had a dog once," he said, "a big, ugly thing. He died."

The chap looked out across the bay. "Three ships out today," he said, taking out a can of beer from somewhere and now openly drinking. Zeno had come back to my side of the bench.

"Boats really," I said, observing that the vessels were only small fishing boats, probably after crabs.

He looked at me, amiable enough. "Ever been at sea?" he asked.

For some reason, I didn't get his meaning. I suppose, with my train of personal thought running along the lines it often does, my first thought was, I've been at sea most of my life.

"I was at sea. On the 'Lord Nelson'," he said. The recollection amused and refreshed him and he jumped up and did a little hornpipe, still being sufficiently careful not to spill any beer. He was not firm on his feet. The cans of strong lager were visible in his coat pockets as he swayed. He wandered away from me, weaving between the other people out for a stroll, singing *A life on the ocean wave* quite loudly.

As he went he paused and looked back at me. "Where's your friend today?" he said and laughed.

Like every seaside town, like every town, I suppose, there are street drinkers. There are people on drugs too, I hear, though I wouldn't know what to look for in those cases. Seaside towns have their own distinct problems arising from the recession and cheap holidays abroad. You can see the social impact. Other coastal towns have it worse than us. The drinkers are more obvious to me, those on the street. Many more, I imagine, drink at home, keep it all behind closed doors. I have seen the regular drinkers, the hardened ones, at the corner shop, at its first opening. A middle-aged man sleeps in one of the shelters on the front, the side facing the sea or the side facing the town, depending on which way the wind is blowing. He is friendly, after a few drinks. Some people chat to him as he takes his early morning tipple. Drinkers or not, they are people after all. I am a little wary. I don't think I am any more or any less sociable to them than I am to anyone else I pass, but something frightens me. There but for the grace of God, etc.

Yvonne, I now believe, drank too much. She liked company and company likes a drink but it went further later on. I don't mind the odd pint but when it becomes a route to forget, to obliterate or to cope with the day, I think it is a problem. Yvonne drank every day. Some days it made her hard and vicious. I never spoke to her about it, though I imagine she knew I didn't quite approve. The reasons she kept to herself. I could understand that her work was often trying and exhausting. A drink to unwind made some sense and was understandable. I had hoped that when she retired it might ease off. Perhaps it had become a habit. Perhaps it had become a dependency. Perhaps it was an illness by then. She drank more if anything; every evening, in and out of company. I don't think it made her any less unhappy. There was a desperate misery to it some days. I didn't like to see it and I don't like to think about it now, looking back.

With Zeno walked, I strolled back up to the seafront to meet Geoff. It was the first time we had met since I was at his house for dinner. When we were settled with our food in front of us I took the opportunity to thank him again for the meal and said how much I had enjoyed it. He said he had enjoyed the evening too and we must do it again soon.

I was feeling as relaxed as I could be in Geoff's company. There had not been a lot of conversation between us but we were like that some days. When we had all but finished our meal, I felt emboldened to ask him about something that had been on my mind, relating to the things he had said about himself that evening when we had met. I didn't want to embarrass him or myself but felt we needed to air the subject a bit if nothing else to show him that I was relaxed about his sexuality.

"I didn't realise you were gay," I said, hopefully in a casual way, not as if it were an issue, just as something a little out of my usual sphere.

"Really?" he said, looking a bit puzzled. "I thought…"

But Geoff didn't finish his thought. I wondered what it was that he thought. That it was obvious? That he thought he had already told me? That he thought someone else might have told me, that it was common knowledge in the community?

"You thought…what?" I asked.

Geoff shrugged his shoulders, hummed a bit. The thought, whatever it was, now lost.

"Well, nothing, I suppose," he said. "It's not a problem, is it?"

"Of course not," I said quickly, "I was glad you were open about it. Just haven't encountered it much personally before."

Geoff laughed. "I doubt that," he said.

He seemed not to know what else to say. And neither did I.

We changed the subject.

When I got back home I gave Zeno a bath. I probably should do it more often than I do but she hates it so much and is so uncooperative into the bargain that I only tackle it about once a month. She has become adept at spotting the signs of an imminent bath as with all the unpleasant things, from her point of view, that she has to endure. She will stay out in the garden; she will hide under the table, as a last resort, she will cower in her crate as if this was some sort of sanctuary it would be wrong for me to invade. Eventually, she will submit and endure the process. I do worry that in her scuffling about in the bath and her attempts to scramble out she might hurt herself. I keep a firm grip and try to deal with the business as quickly as possible. It is worth the effort. That gritty feeling in her coat that you get between baths is gone and replaced with a fluffy smoothness. The colours in her fur stand out, particularly the white bits. And she smells so much nicer. Occasionally, I can't resist burying my nose in her soft pink belly, after her bath, as she licks herself dry.

One thing she does appreciate is the rub down with a towel afterwards. Zeno has always quite enjoyed being towelled down after she has been out in the rain or in the mud. She loves being wrapped up and held close. The noises she makes are close to a purr. After most of the damp has been taken off, she also likes to sit very close and lets me give her a stroke. I know fine well what she is up to. When she finally jumps down, I am damper than she is and she will give herself a vigorous shake and stroll off with a satisfied look.

When it came to making a choice of a dog, right from the start I was looking for a female. Yvonne had no view either way and left the decision to me. In this, she was basically saying that it was up to me; my dog and my responsibility. Yvonne kept herself distant from any decisions in this area, making it clear that I had to take on all the burdens of dog ownership and not involve her.

If I am honest about this, about my choice of a female dog, I suppose I felt that down below, as it were, everything is just so much more neatly organised with a girl. I had known the dogs of relatives, growing up, and even though I was, despite myself, somewhat fascinated by it, I was basically appalled when male dogs would sit on the hearth and lick themselves. Obviously, dogs have no shame about this, it is a ridiculous and unnatural concept but I felt it myself as if somehow my own sexual apparatus was exposed in the dog's act of applying his attention to this area. It was only grooming or at least I hoped it was but it made me excessively uncomfortable. People would make jokey comments as they would if a dog applied itself to your leg, in a sexual manner, with a look of intense concentration on its face.

I had Zeno 'done' in the normal course of things, to avoid unwanted pups and those difficult times of the month. She does still get some attention from other dogs that gets a bit too intimate for my liking, and for hers. Her tail will wrap under her body and she might even give a quick snap if some other dog looks to be taking liberties. It is unlikely that there is anything sexual about this, in the other dog's activity. I know that. I am probably projecting too much of my own perceptions, insecurities and even prejudices onto normal animal behaviour. Where would nature be without it, in any case, without sex?

I have to accept that there is a certain degree of prudery in me. I am that person who does not like to see so much sex on television. Even now that I am on my own, and I can't be embarrassed on behalf of anyone else, I still pull a face and shake my head if anything gets a bit too near the knuckle on television. In my conversation with Geoff when he spoke of his disposition, my main dread had been that he might disclose too much about the bedroom. It is partly my age and upbringing, I suppose. I recall my banishment to bed well before the watershed, even when most other children who were my contemporaries were being gradually exposed to the more adult content of television programming. Not that it ever got so very adult in those days. It would seem very tame indeed today, even to me. Even when I was legitimately of an age when such viewing was permissible, Mother would abruptly turn off the television at any hint of something that appeared to fall within her definition of improper. Though, truth to be told, I was glad she did. The thought of seeing anything of that nature in the context of a family setting was horrifying. Of course, many of my peers, with exactly the same nurturing overcame this parental and even self-censorship quite quickly or so I was led to believe and joined in the new permissiveness with gay abandon.

At the heart of all this, is there a fear of sex or more generally, of sexuality, in whatever context? Perhaps, with Geoff, it is not so much that I am concerned about his homosexuality being brought out into the open for an airing but more a dread of his, mine, or anyone else's sexuality being acknowledged and displayed. I don't recall Yvonne and I having any sort of conversation about our sex life, whether it was satisfactory, what she liked, what I liked. I find even thinking about those questions now very difficult. It has to be said, there were problems at first. I think it was partly the weight of expectation attached to the first time, especially when it has been delayed and deferred for a lengthy period. It makes it too big a thing, particularly when you have scant knowledge of the procedure itself, let alone the anatomy of your partner. Naturally, I assumed any deficiency was down to me. I am not sure it is viewed this way now but then it seemed to me that the man was the active partner, the woman just responded to what was done to her. The man was active, the woman receptive, so if anything was amiss it was the man's fault, without question. I did feel this at the time, that there was a weakness somewhere in me or an absence.

Although it was unsatisfactory at first, I think I did enjoy it, I think Yvonne did enjoy it, and we found a rhythm together in time. Perhaps the most active phase of our sex life did not last as long as that of other couples. But how could I possibly know that one way or the other, when the sex life was a subject off-limits for discussion for me? It was still, however, the impression I had, that other couples did it more often and continued to do it long after that point in our relationship where it had ceased to be a regular thing for Yvonne and me.

I suppose I have to face something at this point. When I spoke of not knowing what to expect, and unfamiliarity with the partner's body, I think I spoke only of myself. I have to acknowledge, to confront, something that I have held as an unarticulated suspicion for some time.

I do not think Yvonne was a virgin when we consummated our marriage.

It was my first time. She said it was her first time. But I don't think it was. I don't think it was even her second or third time.

I was aware and I was prepared for certain physical signs of the loss of virginity. I did not observe them. I know that these are not universally present or always a reliable indicator. But they were absent. This wasn't the main basis for my suspicion. Yvonne was not nervous about our first time; she showed no apprehension or anxiety. Not when I undressed. Not when I uncovered her. Of course, this could have been just an excess of trust, her love for me, knowing that I would be gentle, that this was a journey that we were making together, in faith. But as we joined together, I felt a hint of impatience at my gestures and my caresses. As if my every move had a certain familiarity and nothing of novelty to her. That she was on a pathway she knew well and she was not inclined to linger on the journey, waiting for me to catch up but eager to get to the final destination. I felt a weight of expectation from Yvonne, an element of anticipation, an accommodation to me that I have to say was almost shocking. She touched me in a way that suggested she was familiar with all the ways to manipulate a man. But I must admit that the worst moment came when I caught a glimpse of her face when I drew back from kissing her, from touching her, and what I thought I saw in her face was boredom. My confidence, such as it was, left me immediately. I felt confused and defeated, awkward, clumsy and inept. I paused and drew back until she looked at me directly. She did not ask me what was wrong. She did not encourage me or soothe me or reach out to draw me back to her, with a word or a gesture or a kiss.

We held our position for a little while before I smiled at her as best I could and moved to the other side of the bed, trying not to give any impression, by gesture or expression, that I was unsatisfied or disappointed. My primary concern was that Yvonne did not feel any fault in herself, that all was in order.

We did try again, during our honeymoon, and the outcome improved each time. Perhaps Yvonne had perceived that I lacked confidence and was prepared to move at a pace that we were both comfortable with. I look back and I do believe that if I am correct, if Yvonne had had a lover, potentially more than one lover, before me, if she had been honest about these facts, it would not have mattered to me. We had been so often apart during our college years that it would have been perfectly natural for connections to be made with other people. Perhaps she assumed that I too had experimented during this period. It would not have been unusual for the time and we had made no vows of fidelity, we had made no promises to each other, deliberately so. Perhaps, on this basis, she took the stance that what was in the past was in the past and that our marriage was a fresh start; that neither of us would ask and neither of us would tell. But if she had told me, if she had even suggested that we should just draw a veil over those years, I would have accepted it and moved on very quickly. The thing that rankles with me is that there was deceit involved. It rankles with me that rather than saying nothing she told me that she was a virgin. It is not even that she failed to contradict an assumption I had made. It is my fixed, firm and settled view now, I have a distinct and precise recollection, that she did tell me, and in so many words. She could have kept silent on the matter. I certainly did not ask her about it. She told me. She volunteered that information with no prompting from me.

I cannot smooth over or choose to forget that fact any longer. By it, she put me at a disadvantage, she made me vulnerable, and I cannot now help but feel that something was blighted, something was spoiled, by that act of deceit. It was not an action that arose from love, I feel.

I hadn't realised that almost a month had passed since I had dinner with Geoff. Well, maybe that is not strictly true because I have thought about that evening a lot and my obligation to invite him back. I have let the days go by, not because I didn't want Geoff's company but because I still have no clue as to what to make and how to organise it. I am rusty in the kitchen, to say the least. I knew Geoff would be happy with something simple but I wanted a little more time to do some planning so that everything was right. I am a little in fear of the event, in short. I know I am making more of this than I should. I live simply, Geoff knows that. I have no great kitchen skills, Geoff might guess that. I am not used to having company over nor am I a person with high-level social skills, Geoff must have observed this. So Geoff cannot have very high expectations and I am sure he is more interested in a couple of hours of convivial chat than in cordon bleu cookery and fine wines. Geoff has a little more sophistication than I have, I guess, a bit more knowledge of the world and its finer things but he is pretty much a down to earth chap.

Geoff forced the issue in the end. At breakfast, he mentioned again that he had enjoyed my company over dinner, that it was pleasant for him to get back into the kitchen (Like me, he didn't bother so much when it was just him) and would I like to come over again, soon? I was a bit mortified and felt that I had been rude.

"No," I said, hastily, "you must come to me. I have been meaning to ask."

"Are you sure?" he said. "I don't mind hosting."

"No, it will do me good to make the effort, turn the oven on again and open my house to company. It won't be anything fancy but hopefully, it will be edible. Zeno has never turned her nose up at anything I've shared with her, so it can't be that bad."

"Whatever you make will be fine for me. You don't need to go to a lot of trouble. Not on my account."

So, finally, it is settled and Geoff is to come around on Friday. It's a relief to have it in the diary and it's close enough for me not to get panicked and spend days on preparation. I'll give the house a good clean, it's a good excuse to go from top to bottom for a change. A day to shop and then it will be Friday.

Since I extended my invitation to Geoff, I have been looking at our house with fresh eyes or rather trying to imagine how the house might look to someone else, to Geoff really. There is so much of Yvonne in everything, nothing of me that I can see. I don't exactly know what I mean by that. I couldn't pinpoint too precisely the personality that I identify as mine that is missing from the house. A couple of the rooms are still as Yvonne and I found them when we moved in; the third bedroom, the bathroom. They have a look you associate with a style popular a couple of decades ago but I suspect they were decorated more recently than that. They simply reflect the taste of an older person, with an old-fashioned outlook. Yvonne chose the decoration of the rooms that we did do up. I can't remember even buying the wallpaper or paint or looking at samples or paint charts but I suppose Yvonne must have asked me about it or at least shown me what she had chosen. We got a local man in to do the work. We didn't trust our own skills to make the best job of it and someone recommended this chap.

Is it all a bit feminine? There are a lot of pastel shades about, not an inconsiderable amount of pink also, floral patterns, roses on the walls in the bedroom. Great cabbage roses that do look a lot like cabbages now the colour has faded out of them. Not something I would have chosen but something I have got used to. The whole house reflects Yvonne's taste. There is nothing I find offensive, not much anyway, and what would I replace it with? It must be over six years since the house last saw a paintbrush or a paint roller and the sea air, Zeno's racing about covered in mud and sand and my inattentiveness have taken their toll. When I notice a bit of chipped paint on a door or a scuffed area on a wall, I do occasionally think I should spruce up the place, make it more my own. Yet I identify my taste in negative terms only, what I don't like rather than what I do. I hope I would recognise what I like if I saw it. Perhaps it is just a way of looking, a faculty of observation and appreciation that I have never developed. Women tend to have stronger views about these things.

There is just one area of the house where I recognise my input. Yvonne had identified a very pale carpet that she wanted in the hall and living room. I thought that a vinyl floor would be better in the hall but if had to be carpet I did suggest that a pale colour was not the best option. With Zeno's coming and goings, I thought a darker pattern would show the dirt less. As a solution, Yvonne said that I must always use the backdoor for my walks with Zeno and I must dry her off and clean off the sand and muck before coming through into the house. I must also take my shoes off at the door. Though it would be a bit inconvenient, I did say I would try to do this. I wasn't keen on the idea (Zeno and I always use the front door now; it has more direct access to the road to the beach). My suggestion must have made Yvonne think about her choice, however. She did, in the end, go for a darker carpet. She still put it right into the hall, up to the door. It hasn't worn well but it doesn't show the grime so much.

The decoration of Geoff's house did make a statement, I felt. It was bold in its way, distinctive but I can't fathom the connection between the wallpaper and the Geoff I know. The greys and the blues and the greens might suggest a seaside palette. Was that the thought process, the theme? Or did he just like those colours? Perhaps Geoff's partner was the one with the controlling vision of decor.

Instead of continuing down this road and identifying what changes I could conceivably make to my house, I began to let my thoughts wander, as they tend to do when I am alone. I found myself wondering what proportion of our lives we spend staring at the wallpaper. I don't mean the choosing of the paper, the applying of the paper, the stepping back and admiring the paper, the days or weeks after it is up when we look around and think how much better it is than what was there before. I mean how wallpaper is the foreground or the background to our idle moments.

Sometimes when I sit in the living room, the light fading, letting the thoughts pass through my head, I find my eyes fixed on the wallpaper, I guess for hours on end. I am not exactly actively focused on the wallpaper, I'm focused on my thoughts, if only in a passive way but the pattern is there in front of me, its geometric repetition, the little boxes of graduated sizes going up and down the wall, as my thoughts ascend and descend. I know one little corner of the wall, near the sofa, so well, I stare unblinking so long, that the ghost of that pattern stays on my retina for a while and I find it projected on the carpet, on the curtains, even on Zeno's white patches, when I look away. I think generally that wallpaper fades from consciousness after we have lived with it for even a short while. Isn't wallpaper proverbial for its ability to do that? It's like so many things in my life of late: it takes some catalyst, however unlikely, to make you really notice aspects of the world around you, to think about the things you have taken for granted or just thoughtlessly accepted. To pay attention. To see something that has been submerged or overlooked in all its sudden and bright reality.

Geoff came round to dinner last night. He arrived promptly, bearing the usual gifts of courtesy. I had said that he should bring Bella with him and she bounded off immediately with Zeno. We had both greeted them at the door.

Geoff had asked me earlier in the week what I intended to cook, presumably so he could match the wine he was going to bring to the food that I planned to serve. So I had to come up with something on the spur of the moment. In a way, this was a good thing. I hadn't had time to look through Yvonne's cookbooks to settle on something a bit more elaborate. I hadn't had time to plan or shop or fret about it. Instead, I just said, off the top of my head 'a casserole' something familiar and safe. It just popped into my head. Geoff had asked chicken or red meat. I said red meat. It offered more scope, I thought, and chicken can be a bit boring and easy to overcook. You can keep a beef casserole stewing all day and it won't harm it.

Geoff had a quick look round the house when he arrived and conscious of my earlier musings about it, I immediately apologised for its state, said that I intended to redecorate, give it a bit of a make-over. Of course, I had spent most of the day cleaning it, so I felt easy enough on that score.

"But why?" he said. "I like your house, how you have done it. It's all in keeping. You might need to do a bit of touching up, and there, I can see that, wear and tear and all that. But I wouldn't change it radically. It still has its character; it's lived in and liveable. You can kick your shoes off and put your feet up. I wish we'd done less to our house, kept its structure at least. It's more Jim's taste than mine. He wanted something modern and clean. I like to feel comfortable at home, not worrying about where you can put a cup down or muddy paw prints on the lino. If anything my house looks more dated than yours, it's so much of the taste of that particular point in time."

I looked around and could not quite see Geoff's perspective. Yvonne would not have seen the house the way Geoff did. She would have thought that it had been styled in the best of taste, classic and timeless. Comfort had not been the primary theory behind it. Yvonne might also have thought that Geoff's description implied that the house was a bit scruffy, dilapidated and far from pristine. But Geoff's comments did put me at ease somewhat. I began to think that perhaps the house had moulded itself more around me and Zeno since Yvonne died, more than I realised. The cushions, those that I had kept or Zeno hadn't had a go at, were no longer strategically placed. There were fewer ornaments. The glass vases that once cluttered the windowsills were now under the sink. The pot plants had all died off. Furniture had been reorganised more for functionality than to align with some aesthetic principle of design. The couch faced the television set and the coffee table was now situated so that you could actually rest a coffee cup down on it. Overall, the house had relaxed a bit, in a sense. It no longer had to be on its best behaviour all the time.

 I only had beer to offer to Geoff. I couldn't vouch for any of the other alcohol in the house so I didn't mention it. We saved his wine for dinner and actually I thought it was OK. The casserole was good enough, I thought, and I had bought the dessert so couldn't take any credit for that. Everything felt convivial and Zeno didn't disgrace me by begging at the table. We lingered over coffee, talking about this and that.

 "How did you meet Jim?" I asked Geoff at one point. It still felt strange saying Geoff's partner's name.

 "In a bar," said Geoff, "in Fort Ness."

 At first, I thought that was all Geoff wanted to say about the matter but I think he was wondering how much to tell me and how to phrase it. Perhaps there was something a bit sordid about the circumstances, I wondered. In due course, he continued.

 "Jim was working at the university. He was a marine biologist. I had a job in the library at the same university as Jim, mainly admin at first; issuing books, stamping books, shelving books. I started straight after graduation; an English degree, fits you for nothing, not even reading. I still can't break the habit of reading with a pencil in my hand. You lose the plot, quite literally, in the detail; the grammar, the punctuation, the adjectives, why this word and not that word. I had hoped to subject specialise in the library in time but I ended up spending years and years helping with the computerisation of the catalogue. That was where I was when I met Jim."

 Geoff paused. "I suppose Jim picked me up." Geoff looked at me, to see how I was reacting to this but I kept my expression as blank as I could, keeping my thoughts to myself. "It went as those things often went, for both of us. It could have been just a one-off thing, I suppose. I don't think either of us was actively looking for anything else at that time. I gathered that Jim had been a bit wild up to this point. He was definitely on the prowl. I was more ambivalent. It wouldn't have bothered me just to have a drink and go home by myself. I liked gay bars for the atmosphere and company. Jim was out for a specific reason."

I hoped at this point that Geoff was not going to go into too much detail about this initial liaison but he passed over it quickly.

"I guess the timing was right, I guess we clicked somehow. On the surface, we hadn't that much in common. He was a little older than me. Physically, he wasn't the type I usually went for. His taste was more inclusive, as it were, no 'types' were ruled in or ruled out for him. But I liked him, on a human level. There was a warmth about him, nothing aggressive or predatory, just a friendliness. He made me laugh and he smelled nice, I recall. Maybe there was a hint of the sea on his person, the outdoors at any rate." Geoff was watching me, wondering I think whether he should make his next remark. "The sex was good."

Geoff might have noticed that I raised my eyebrows at this point, I was a little alarmed. He did not elaborate and I breathed again.

"Well, anyway, we both wanted to see each other again and it went from there. I moved in with him after only a couple of months. There was an element of convenience to it. The lease on my flat was up and I had been looking for a new place. But we both wanted it and my impending homelessness just forced the issue a little. We never regretted it. Neither of us went to gay bars after that. I think there is a natural lifespan for that youthful hedonism and it can look a bit sad, still trawling the bars after a certain age. Happily, we both had reached that point, where we wanted a different carry-on. We were very happy. We got married a couple of years before he died."

I asked Geoff how he came to Cornubay.

"Jim was a malacologist," he said, "he studied molluscs; squid, whelks, winkles and so on. Don't ask me to explain too much. Many creatures without much appeal to me fascinated Jim. I prefer creatures to have a face, to get my sympathy. After we got together, he was relocated to the marine station up by Spar Point, near the lighthouse. This coastline has several unique species of sea slugs and it was ideal for him and his research. He was teaching less by then and focusing more on his research. It was convenient to have a base nearer to the marine station. We looked around various places around here and decided to move to Cornubay because it looked civilised and well placed for various reasons. I got a job in the library here, only part-time but enough to make a contribution. We were settled. When Jim's parents died, we had enough money to pay off the mortgage, so things were comfortable."

I told Geoff how I had met Yvonne.

"Childhood sweethearts," he said. I didn't think that term applied but accepted it.

It occurred to me that the trajectory of Geoff's life and my life had followed very different arcs and how remarkable it was, in a way that they had crossed at this point. Most people I knew had lived similar lives at bottom. Maybe children had come along, maybe there were a few divorces along the way. But the building blocks were the same, the core elements. I saw Geoff as a very different person to myself but perhaps that was an over-simplification. We had ended up in the same boat, after all, alone in our later years. I found him easy to talk to and I don't often find that.

"When did you retire?" I asked him.

"I haven't," he said, "not quite. I still do shifts at the library, just a couple of evenings now, five until eight. It brings in a little extra. I still receive a bit of a spouse's pension, from Jim's work. He died before he retired so there was quite a large lump sum due to me as his partner. Just as well we had married or I would have missed out. I have a work pension myself, not a lot, due to start in a couple of years. Occasionally, I dip into the capital I have left, for extras. But generally, I manage quite comfortably. I don't really need to work but I enjoy it, mixing with people and colleagues, getting out of the house for a purpose."

I was a little surprised by this. I had no idea that Geoff still had a job, albeit part-time. But then he is a little younger than me and why wouldn't he keep at a job if he enjoyed it. I had not known that he and Jim had been married either, though of course, I knew that this is a thing these days. Geoff had not referred to Jim as his 'husband', incongruous as that would have sounded to my ears. It was always 'partner'. There was the ring, of course, and that had formed the basis of my misguided assumptions about him, that he was a widower, with a deceased wife. Are men who lose a 'husband' still called widowers, I wondered. People of the same sex can and do marry, I hear, but I had never met or known of anyone in this position. I wondered a little if Geoff kept the status of his relationship with Jim a little shady deliberately. Did his neighbours know about it, I wondered, his work colleagues? Cornubay is a small town, a backwater, really. Who knows what people behind the twitching curtains would think? Why would you draw attention to it unnecessarily? But then he and Jim presumably lived together quite openly. It was all very strange to me.

Now that Geoff had broached the subject of his sexuality so openly, I found I had questions about it. He must have been asked these questions many times before; how did you know you were gay? When did you know? But Geoff was patient when he answered them.

"How do straight people know they are straight?" he said. "When do they know? It's like asking when did you know that you had red hair or blue eyes. You know when you look, when you draw it to the attention of yourself or it is forced upon your attention as something that marks a difference to another person. That question is sometimes phrased as, when did you 'realise' that you were gay. That's maybe a better way to put the question. When did it become real, enter consciousness? The answer is the same, straight or gay, that realisation starts around the same time and in the same way. You find you knew all along. It's all about the moment that you let it become part of your thinking self. It comes at different times to different people. Many straight people, possibly some gay people, never bring it forward into consciousness. They are just who they are and don't have occasion to define it in any more detailed way than that. For gay people, there is a little more pressure or incentive to acknowledge who you are. It usually takes a little more effort to find a way to express it, become it. You probably notice this fact of life at the same time as you realise that you are different to the majority if it isn't itself the reason for you realising the difference. But we are all different, perhaps every sexuality is unique."

I didn't engage further in this topic with Geoff. I didn't want it to dominate the conversation, make it seem bigger than it needed to be. I think I still had more questions. I think I disagreed with some of the things he had said. But I respected Geoff's honesty.

We turned to other topics and we finished Geoff's wine before he left. Bella and Zeno were both asleep by then and Bella was reluctant to be roused. Geoff thanked me for the evening and the food and slipped Bella onto her lead. Zeno joined me as I saw Geoff out. It looked very dark outside. I hadn't realised it had got so late. I watched Geoff as he walked down the street, right to the point where he disappeared around the bend in the road. I switched off the lights, locked the door and went to bed.

I do relish my daily walks with Geoff. It's like seeing things anew. I will notice something and point it out to Geoff; a pheasant in a bare field, perhaps, looking out of place and bewildered, conspicuous and exposed, the opposite of blending in. How nature sustains such a vain and stupid bird, I will never know, probably because the female of the species got all the brains. The males are more beautiful, however. Make of that what you will.

Geoff has profited from his time with Jim. He is much more knowledgeable about the coast and its creatures. He will remark to me about a shell on the beach and tell me about the creature who lived in it. A squiggle of sand he will identify as some sort of worm or its tracks. Geoff will see life where I just see sand and pebbles. It's good to have this interchange, this dialogue, as we go; an active engagement with the environment and with each other.

Since we had become regular dog walking companions, Geoff and I decided to have the odd excursion, further afield, whilst the weather still held. I can't remember who suggested it. I think we had been talking about the places we liked around the area. I mentioned somewhere that Geoff had not been to and he mentioned a few places that I had not yet visited. It seemed like a good idea to have a few days out, to share these places and even explore local areas that neither of us knew. We would plan it so that there was somewhere we could take the dogs and somewhere to have a bite to eat, on the way there or on the way back. It seemed like a natural step forward.

We kicked around a number of ideas for where to go for our first trips out, places that one or the other of us had visited nearby that might be worth another visit and some entirely new to both of us. We went to a Tudor manor house as our first excursion, a little way inland from us. The house itself was closed when we got there, its main season already over but we walked around the grounds or at least those areas where dogs were allowed; the period knot gardens, courtyards and topiary featured lawns. We found a cafe on the way back and it was an enjoyable day on the whole. We had a drive out into the countryside the second time, to see a small lake in a secluded spot. It was very peaceful. Not a soul about. Some of the trees surrounding the lake were showing the first signs of autumn colour. We had lunch at a little pub on the way, though we both found the food disappointing. After our meal, Bella was sick in the car park and Geoff was eager to set off back home. I was glad that we were in Geoff's car in case there was another incident on the way back. We had all the windows down. Zeno was having a great time. Bella sulked and pouted.

All this was quite pleasant in a way, if a little staid but not without disappointments.

Then we had a very different sort of day. That was yesterday.

I have to say that I still have a little bit of a buzz about me, from our day out yesterday. I think I can cheerfully say that I had fun, with no reservations. I am still processing my feelings about this and wondering why there is a small element of guilt in amongst them. It's down to Yvonne, I suppose. But why on earth would taking a little pleasure in life still make me feel a fraction of a degree of betrayal of her memory. Will I, should I, forever hereafter believe that my bedrock emotion post-Yvonne has to be the sadness of her loss and keeping faith with that? I am sure Yvonne wouldn't have moped about if I had been the first to go. I wouldn't have wanted her to. And I doubt that she would have expected me to bury myself in grief for the rest of my life. Partly I suppose it relates to the fact that although Yvonne enjoyed the company of many people and found satisfaction in a range of pursuits that did not often include me, my sole source of joy in life was Yvonne, up to a few years ago, and for many years before then. I have come to the decision that this feeling is a stupid, irrational and life-limiting emotion. I am resolved that I won't let it spoil or taint anything again.

After the rather ambivalent trips we had made in a few short days, I had not expected Geoff to suggest another outing so soon. On our morning walk, Geoff seemed excited; he had something to tell me. He waited until we had completed our circuits before he explained.

Geoff had finally said to me, "I have a plan."

I had a brief moment of apprehension. "I hope you aren't going to suggest something spontaneous," I said, "I need a few days' notice to be spontaneous." I meant it as a joke, and Geoff took it that way but I fear it contained more than a grain of truth. I have always liked to plan and prepare for social engagements.

"Don't worry. I am not suggesting we do anything on the spur of the moment. Not today, at any rate. But let's not delay. The weather is bound to take a turn for the worse soon."

What Geoff suggested was that we should have a day out in Cornubay but not as our usual selves but as 'holidaymakers'. The season was petering out, we were already in September, and soon the seasonal attractions and venues would begin to close. As residents, we avoided the holiday crowds (Well, there were rarely crowds, as such). We kept ourselves separate from the more heightened sensations of the summer holidays. We did not eat at thronging outlets, we did not go on the popular end of the beach, we skirted around the amusement arcades, we walked our dogs early, when it was still quiet, and we looked forward to the time when we would get our more sedate and picturesque town back. Although Cornubay has held back a little from the more full-on seaside extravaganza, in all its gaudy display, areas of the town do have more of this aspect in the summer months. The pier opens up its small fairground, the doors of the two arcades are wide open, the small kiosks on the front begin to dispense the traditional coastal fare and the air is redolent with the smell of frying onions and burning sugar.

What a shame, Geoff reasoned, to live in a seaside town and never have the seaside 'experience', to never encounter the place as visitors do. He explained that it would give us a different perspective on the town. And it could be a laugh. I could see his point.

We agreed that we would meet on Friday, weather permitting (Though rain is as much a seaside tradition as candyfloss, in my experience). Under the clock, we decided, as holiday folk did of yore. We would give our dogs a long, early walk, not intending to bring them with us.

As I walked along the front, towards our meeting point, I did begin to feel that almost childlike sense of anticipation. The town had begun to feel like a different place already, as I tried to view it as a visitor might. I became much more aware of the sensations of the seaside, the plinking and chatter from the machines in the amusement arcade, the smell of bacon and burgers cooking, even the colours seemed brighter. I spotted Geoff from afar. He had embraced the seaside theme more enthusiastically than I had. He was wearing his shorts, a gaudy shirt and pink sunglasses. He did not seem the least bit self-conscious and in the spirit of the day, he gave me a brief hug as we met.

"Glad to see you made an effort," he said. Of course, I hadn't, apart from going back into shorts for the occasion and wearing sandals with no socks. But I was up for whatever came along.

The day was perfect, very warm for the time of year. The tide was in and there were more people on the sands than there had been for a while. We went to join them.

I drew the line at building sandcastles but we did paddle, eating candyfloss as we went. The sand between my toes felt glorious, as if a novel sensation; as if I had never walked on sand before or felt the cold of the sea as it lapped over my foot. There may have been glances askance from passers-by; two old men acting like fools. But neither of us were bothered. Geoff kicked a bit of seawater up at me. I kicked back but almost fell over.

"Would this have been the kind of day that Jim would have enjoyed?" I asked.

"God, no," said Geoff, "he would have been mortified. He avoided this part of town as if there was a plague outbreak here. What about Yvonne?"

"Not on your life," I said, "too grand for anything like this." It was out of my mouth before I could stop it. But it was completely true, I realised.

"Well, it is lucky we found each other. Come on, let's have a bevvy."

We sauntered on and found ourselves in a pub near the front, popular with visitors. It was only eleven o'clock, but there were already punters inside and in the beer garden. We found a gloomy corner indoors, near the jukebox.

"It's a bit early, isn't it?" I said, the old habit of caution creeping in.

Geoff gave me a look. "But we're on holiday, Paul," he said. This was the first time that Geoff had used my name when addressing me. I wondered, in passing, whether this had significance. Geoff went to the bar to get our drinks.

The pint that Geoff had bought me went a little to my head. I was already light-headed and the slightest thing was making me giggle. Geoff put some old song on the jukebox. Something about charabancs, Ferris wheels, brass bands and cider. I felt nostalgic all of a sudden and could have got maudlin if I had been alone. I bought another round as we tried but failed, to pace ourselves. The day was rushing at us.

We went for fish and chips and ate them hot out of the paper, sitting on the front. They tasted more delicious than I could have imagined; salt and vinegar in abundance, almost chapping my lips. I had intended to save a bit of fish for Zeno but it was gone before I knew it and I licked my fingers to get every last scrap of taste out of the paper. Geoff binned the wrappers and we sat for a long while, digesting, just admiring the view, the sea blurring into a golden haze. We commented now and then on the people passing by, speculating on their stories, wondering where they came from and what lives they would go back to.

After our little rest, we went back up along the front and onto the pier. There was a small, seasonal funfair at the end of the pier, still open but not many people about. We had a look around. It was mainly kiddies' rides; a helter-skelter, a few stalls, a dainty merry-go-round that looked to be old, even though freshly painted. Victorian? Edwardian? I had no idea. That fairground organ music played from somewhere, on a tape, I imagine these days. Geoff might have wanted to have a go on a ride but I dissuaded him. I doubted that they would have let him on, though some parents were riding with their children. We threw a few balls at moving targets (Do those booths have a name?) but didn't win anything. I was sharply reminded of childhood holidays whilst we looked around. There is an instant connection in places like this, it touches you like a current, throws you back immediately.

The arcade near the pier was a much more modern structure, the games of recent date, many involving shooting and killing which I found a little disturbing. There were a few retro pieces, taking old coins that you could buy at a kiosk. I put a few pennies in for old time's sake, losing all of them. I pulled the pins that sent a ball rattling around a spiral. I watched the cherries spin and fail to align. I added to the accumulation of coins being swept and pushed to a precipice but never quite cascading over. There was a machine that told fortunes but I didn't want to know my future and neither did Geoff. The pinball machines too were as I remembered from childhood. We both had a go at pulling the chrome knob that sprang a ball into the machine. Mine just seemed to catch at the top of the game and then roll back. Geoff had better luck but came nowhere near the top points score.

Inflation seemed to have operated in a significant way in the arcade. Many machines now had a minimum stake of fifty pence or even a pound. I found that a bit steep. Despite this, I was soon dropping in coins without restraint. My father always hated these machines. He said he did not like to spend money quicker than he could earn it. I took after my mother and could only afterwards reflect that there was something thrilling about slotting good money after bad.

I told Geoff of an incident in my childhood when I spent all my holiday money in about twenty minutes in an arcade, where my parents had left me when they went to buy tickets for a show. It was totally addictive and exhilarating. My sister, who had gone with them, taunted me for my stupidity. My father said I might as well have pushed my pennies through the gaps in the flooring on the pier, into the sea. Later, when Mother took pity on me and gave me a few shillings for me to spend, I went back onto to the front on my own, not to lose my money again in the arcades but to drop my pennies through the wooden planks of the pier. My father had been sort of right. I got just as much pleasure wasting my money by seeing it slide through the slats of the pier, seeing it twist and plummet into the churning sea below. I was not totally witless though and I did keep back a few coins to buy rock. When Geoff asked me if I wanted to push some more pennies through the pier that day I told him not to be so daft.

It was well past noon when I recalled Zeno and felt that we must reluctantly go back and let the dogs out.

I had a restless night after our seaside day, as I said, but in the morning, I took Zeno out and met up with Geoff. He still seemed to have a little bit of a glow about him from the previous day, almost a fever on him. He looked to have caught a little of the sun, his eyes darted about and he was smiling broadly. I had been inclined to revert to our everyday reserve but he hugged me and said how much he had enjoyed our jaunt.

Perhaps the experiences of the previous day had brought us closer, co-conspirators (Though against what I had not yet fathomed), even to the extent of closing a physical and social distance between us. Geoff's hug did not throw me as it could have once. My parents were not physically demonstrative of affection, which was not unusual for the time. This is not to say there was no love in the household. These days, people do show their feelings, their emotions, more and not just in a family or private setting. Some of it does not always appear genuine to me. But growing up there were no hugs, no kisses, not many tears. The only time I can recall Mother kissing me, at any point in my life, was on my wedding day, with a formal kiss on the cheek, something ceremonial almost. My sister kissed both parents on the cheek, when she visited them after we had grown up. My father seemed to appreciate it; my mother endured it. My mother made it clear with relatives and friends that she did not kiss men, other than her husband; women, which I assume included my sister, were allowed to kiss her cheek if they initiated it. I rarely saw my parents kiss. My father occasionally kissed my mother, on the lips, when he went to work and she tolerated this. My sister and I were always a bit fascinated when we witnessed this, any leaking through of the notion that there was real affection there. Of course, there must have been, at least at some time. It looked a bit awkward and unfamiliar to them, however. We felt as if we were seeing something that we shouldn't, something not for public observation.

Though I had resolved that my marriage would be different, that through gestures I would show Yvonne often that I loved her, she did not particularly respond as I hoped she might, did not spontaneously reciprocate. We kissed good morning most days and good night before we turned over to sleep but there was something perfunctory about it, a sense of an obligation as our marriage matured. In the early days, things had been different.

I have always lavished Zeno with affectionate attention, almost indecently so, you might think. I pet and nuzzle her endlessly, snuffle her neck, kiss her forehead, stroke her ears and shoulders, and even find myself drawn to bury my face in her stomach when she rolls on her back and shows her pink, vulnerable, almost hairless belly. In return, she licks my face and my hands and my head and my neck, especially after a haircut, when the barber has buzzed away the stray hairs on the back of my neck and it is a little stubbly.

Geoff it seems has surrendered more to the habits of the age and goes in for hugs. Perhaps, with his persuasion, he has fewer inhibitions about physical proximity to another man. Perhaps that's just how he is, how he was brought up to be. It would feel wrong to pull back a little, hold myself at a distance, under these circumstances. I would not want him to feel embarrassed or self-conscious about it. I can see that this is how it will be now.

It occurred to me that Geoff and I do not interact with each other's dogs as we do with our own. He is as fond of Bella, I can see, as I am of Zeno. He pets and hugs her and spoils her but has not even so much as patted Zeno as I recall. Nor have I with Bella. The dogs are quite different; they have different diets, different temperaments, and different routines. Bella sticks with Geoff, Zeno sticks with me. Zeno never goes to Geoff for a treat or any show of affection, and Bella never comes to me. I have noticed though that they are consorting more freely with each other than they did initially. Perhaps the dogs have consulted together and come to the view that the other owner is the rival for their master's affections, and not the owner's dog.

Our next outing, a week or so after the seaside 'experience' as Geoff called it, did not turn out to be an unqualified success. At least there ended up being a touch of melancholy about it.

Geoff had suggested that we should have a trip up towards the marine station where Jim had worked. I had visited the area near the lighthouse, on the point, but the station was about two miles further up the coast and it overlooked a rather lovely, secluded cove, so Geoff said.

It was not the best day to start with, the morning we set out. There had been fog first thing and this had given way to heavy rain that only gradually eased to a light drizzle. Geoff was driving, as he knew the way but we ended up down a muddy track, with potholes and brambles edging it. I could not believe that this track lead anywhere and as it turned out, it didn't really. When we got to our planned destination, it was obvious that the place had been abandoned, maybe for some years. The marine station was still there but it was in a poor state. The weather and the sea salt had very rapidly impacted the structure. The windows and doors were boarded over, the land around it overgrown. There was even a half-filled skip to one side of the building. It was a depressing spot, an unloved limb of the coast.

"It must be the university cuts," Geoff said, looking visibly upset, as if a part of his life with Jim had been blighted and left neglected, along with the structure of the station.

From my casual viewing, the building itself did not look as if it had been built to last. It seemed flimsy and insubstantial, particularly in such an exposed part of the coast. The cliffs up there did not look too stable either, and the unit appeared to have been built far too close to the edge. Or perhaps erosion had caught up with it more rapidly than originally anticipated.

We let the dogs out of the car to stretch their legs but I didn't let Zeno off the lead and I kept her well away from both the building and the cliff edge. I could foresee the whole lot going off the edge, onto the rocks and into the sea, within a couple of winters.

Geoff tried to make the best of it and said there was a way down the cliff into the little cove, on the side of the promontory towards the lighthouse. Access looked a bit doubtful to me but we made our way towards the edge and down some little steps cut into the cliff, reinforced with wooden slats. Halfway down, a landslip seemed to have taken away the remaining steps but it was a gentle slope and a rough path took us to the beach. Geoff had been right in this case. It was a beautiful, isolated and sheltered spot, the sand very yellow, the shallow waves coming in very gently, catching the weak sun that peeped through occasionally. It did not look as if this little spit of coast was much visited. The turning tide could easily cut off access to the route back up the cliff, for the unwary.

We let the dogs off the lead and they sniffed about. There was very little breeze in the shelter of the cove and the cliff sides captured the sun. It felt a good few degrees warmer on the beach than up on the top of the cliff.

"It would be great to have a swim here," Geoff said, as we walked up to where the waves were breaking.

"I don't have my swimming trunks with me," I said.

"Does it matter? It's like our own private beach."

Geoff was joking, I think, but I wasn't sure.

"I don't think I'm quite ready for that," I said.

"You're probably right to be wary. It's likely to be much colder in there than it looks."

I nodded, keeping an eye on the dogs, who had found something alive and were half intrigued, half wary of it. A crab, I think.

"I do like to swim, though," I said, "in the summer months."

"Thinking about it, I don't know if I have ever had a proper swim in the sea here, never been in above my ankles."

"You should come with me. I think we'll have a few more mild days before autumn sets in properly, and the temperature of the water is still quite accommodating."

Geoff's mood seemed to have lifted a little but it was only on the surface. His eyes kept drifting up to the abandoned marine station.

"I think I recall now that it was only meant to be temporary," he said.

Most things are, I thought to myself.

Geoff called Bella over to him and stroked her ears. Zeno came to me too, without being called. It was time to go. The sun had slipped behind a cloud and looked set to remain out of view. It changed the character of the little cove as if the year had suddenly pivoted into a new and grimmer season.

The way back up the cliff looked more hazardous, from the bottom, the pathway to safety less distinct. We clipped the dogs back onto their leads, as if in silent accord, and headed back. Part of the plan had been for us to go to the lighthouse after the marine station and maybe get something to eat on the way. But the day had grown a bit sombre, the skies darkly clouded, threatening more rain, and neither of us suggested prolonging the day. We each kept our thoughts to ourselves on the drive back.

I have not seen so much of Geoff over the past week. He has a friend staying with him, arrived Saturday afternoon. Someone Geoff knew from a while ago, Stewart, he said he was called. Stewart had been living abroad, teaching, I think, somewhere in Europe. I didn't catch all the details when Geoff told me.

Geoff was all for continuing our routine whilst Stewart visited, meeting for breakfast, our walks and so on, with his friend accompanying us some of the time. I decided against this, to give Geoff space and let him focus on hosting his friend. Geoff looked a bit disappointed at that but I didn't want to intrude and Geoff understood.

It has thrown me a bit, though, not having Geoff with me on our daily walks. I skipped the Tuesday breakfast altogether. It would not have seemed right breakfasting alone now, and I did also wonder if Geoff might be there with Stewart. I decided it was best to avoid it completely. I have spent more time indoors this week than I have for some time.

I saw Geoff and someone I assumed was Stewart out walking Bella one morning, during his friend's stay. They were in the distance, on the beach, whilst I was with Zeno. I am pretty sure that neither of them had seen me. They were walking quite slowly, deep in conversation but I had no intention of catching up with them, not wishing to disturb them. I didn't really want to meet Stewart. I was happy to just observe them from afar. Unfortunately, Zeno had spotted Bella and was eager to catch up. She began to tug at the lead, spurring me on, and finally let out a couple of sharp barks, to get Bella's attention. Bella recognised the barks and halted and began to pull Geoff towards me. I don't think Geoff would have known Zeno's bark and it took a while before he lifted his head from his conversation and looked down at Bella and then back towards me. I stopped dead, making as if I was about to turn about and head home. Geoff was still a way off, so I raised a hand in greeting but held my ground. Geoff looked back at me and waved himself. He was waiting to see if I would catch up with him but I pulled Zeno towards me, turned around and we walked back down the beach.

Zeno was straining on the lead, pulling me towards Bella and Geoff. I felt a little conflicted as I tugged Zeno to heel and headed home.

Perhaps this was all a little rude of me. I have wondered since why I was reluctant to meet Stewart, why I had not shown more interest when Geoff told me about his guest coming to stay, why I did not really want to know more about Stewart, why I did not ask Geoff how he knew him and what their relationship was, past or present. It would have been polite and to be honest, I was curious. Of course, I suspected an ex. Before Jim? During Geoff's time with Jim, after Jim? I was afraid of discovering something murky, something I might find a bit distasteful or at least uncomfortable. But why I jumped to this conclusion, and why I thought it was anything like my business, to the extent that I could have concerns about the connection, I don't know. Stewart could have been a former work colleague, a family friend, anyone really.

From the distance that I had viewed them, Stewart seemed a man younger than Geoff, a good deal younger than me. He was slim and very tall so that he had to bend down close to Geoff to catch his words, on a big expanse of open beach with the waves breaking beside them. They were near enough to be touching, I thought, hunched, close at shoulder level as if to make a break for the wind. Their interaction, heads close together, seemed to betoken a much more intense and private conversation than any I had experienced with Geoff.

Was Stewart good-looking? Too far away to tell and how should I judge?

Geoff texted me a couple of times during the week. He didn't mention Stewart.

I will be glad when things are back to normal.

Stewart left Cornubay on Thursday afternoon and Geoff texted me to ask if he could pop around on Thursday evening. I said it was fine. Obviously, I had no plans. I had not seen either Geoff or Stewart again during the period of Stewart's visit. It is possible that I might have subconsciously slightly altered my schedule, taking Zeno out a little earlier and so on, to avoid another encounter. I should give some thought to that, I expect.

When Geoff arrived, we settled down on the sofa. I offered Geoff coffee or a beer. He chose the coffee. I have re-familiarised myself with the operation of a cafetière because I know this is how Geoff prefers it and I keep in the house the blend of coffee that he buys, to be hospitable. I will sometimes have a cup with Geoff myself, though I prefer tea, otherwise there is often too much left over and I don't like throwing it away. He had left Bella back at his house.

I asked how the visit with Stewart had gone and Geoff said it had been good to see him again, after a break of about four years. I found out a little more about Stewart from Geoff. Apparently, although Stewart did some teaching work, his primary job was as a translator for the EU, in Brussels, where he lived. It sounded like an interesting job. I didn't quite discover how Stewart and Geoff knew each other (And I didn't ask directly) but they had known each other for some years and Stewart had visited Cornubay once before when Jim was still alive.

Geoff asked me how I was, what I had been up to. He seemed concerned about me for some reason, that I had all but disappeared for the week. I had been fine, I told him, taken the opportunity of time on my hands to crack on with a few jobs around the house that I had been putting off. This wasn't really true but I didn't want Geoff feeling sorry for me or thinking that I couldn't get by for a week on my own. Geoff said he was glad that I had kept occupied. He had missed our meetings. We sat side by side, sipping our coffee, and Geoff was silent for a few minutes.

"You could have joined us, you know, for some of the time," Geoff said, turning to me. "I think you would have liked Stewart. He's good company."

I shrugged. Geoff was looking at me, frowning but I didn't say anything.

"He's just a friend," said Geoff.

I shrugged again. Geoff's friendships were not really my concern.

We left the topic of Stewart there and I asked Geoff if he wanted a top-up of coffee. Geoff said he would and he followed me, holding his cup, into the kitchen. He put a hand on my shoulder, standing beside me, as I poured.

"It's a good brew," he said, "I think you have got the hang of it now."

I joined him in another cup of coffee and we sat down again. Zeno had taken our place on the sofa. I tucked in beside her and Geoff took a chair, not wishing to disturb her.

"Are we back on for our walk tomorrow?" Geoff asked. "I think Bella has missed Zeno."

"I think Zeno felt Bella's absence too. So, yes, it will be great to have our joint walks back. Dogs like their routines," I said, "change can unsettle and confuse them."

"I guess so," said Geoff. He might have been thinking that my remarks applied equally to me.

He stayed for another half hour but then said his goodbyes, seeing as we were getting close to nine o'clock and he knew I generally retired around then.

I forgot Yvonne's birthday this year. Or at least I forgot to remember Yvonne's birthday. It has been one of those dates, passing each year, when I remember Yvonne. It still is but it is not a day with particularly strong associations for me, such as our wedding anniversary and the date of Yvonne's death. Yvonne was not one for celebrating birthdays, we never did anything special. I always bought her a card and some flowers, and there were cards from other friends and family members. But Yvonne did not encourage this and did not share the date with many people. I suppose, if you make a fuss, if you let people know it is your birthday, if you have a party or go out to celebrate, the question that always follows is, how old are you, or worse, is it a big one. I was always taught it is rude to ask a lady's age and I think Yvonne in this respect was of that old school of thinking, especially as the years accumulated.

In the early years, we often went out for a meal for Yvonne's birthday. I used to buy her a present, nothing too expensive but just something to show I cared. One year, some weeks before her birthday, Yvonne suggested a different arrangement, to save me the bother of choosing (And presumably getting it wrong). She had a new handbag and said that this was what I had bought her for her birthday. It did look very Yvonne. Not something I could have possibly chosen. So it seemed right. It was a bit more expensive than I might have stretched to but I think this might have been her thirtieth birthday so that made sense. This continued for a little while until we came to an understanding that I should just give Yvonne an agreed sum of cash money in future and she could spend it how she wanted on her birthday. I did ask her from time to time what she had bought but she tended to be a bit vague, so I stopped asking. There was no reciprocal arrangement as regards to my birthday. But that was fine for me. I had everything I needed. I hated a big fuss. Yvonne never forgot to buy me a card, though, and always asked if I wanted to do anything special on the day. I was happy just to have a night in and spend the time with her. Since Yvonne died, I don't get cards. My sister Barbara did use to send one, and I always remembered hers, her husband's and the children's birthdays (Now grown men, I suppose) but it has petered out of late. They move about a lot with Gordon's job (Her husband). I think I have their latest address somewhere but I couldn't be sure.

I missed not buying something for Yvonne on her birthday. I did spend a lot of time choosing something special, to surprise her. But I think most chaps struggle to get inside a woman's head, to identify the perfect gift, unless the wife drops heavy hints. I always bought flowers, though. You can't go far wrong with flowers.

Geoff's birthday is in February; he is an Aquarius. I know this because he told me. Jim was a Leo; Yvonne must have been Scorpio, whatever any of that means. Ridiculous for a grown man, an educated man, like Geoff, to know these things or give it any credence, I thought. There was probably an element of tongue-in-cheek about it I guessed when we had this discussion; a bit of fun. My mother had a thing about reading the future in tea leaves and she was well versed in the etiquette of greeting single magpies. I have habitually avoided walking under ladders but that must have a practical health and safety basis. I wouldn't reach for astrology to make sense of the world. Of all the schemes, natural or supernatural that are available, it seems to me that the most unlikely way to discern a plan, to identify the order in the chaos around us. Our fate cannot be in the stars, in my mind.

Some, I know, do set store by horoscopes. I remember once when I was on an interview panel when I was working. We had an over-abundance of good candidates and we were at a stalemate as to who to appoint. One panel member, in all seriousness I thought at the time, checked out their star signs from their application forms, to inform our choice. Might as well have tossed a coin, I offered. The others who were interviewing took this suggestion at face value and we wasted ten minutes or so, debating the merits of Virgo over Pisces, as a fit with the team. I honestly could not tell during this if we had all gone a bit mad or just needed a change of head, a bit of a distraction from the serious business before us. I have to think now that the initial suggestion was a joke. But who knows?

I still have two minds about how Geoff views it all. He does seem to know an awful lot about it. He asked me quite early on when my birthday was and said straight away, "Ah, Libra; that makes sense." He didn't elaborate at the time, how the random stellar configuration at my birth had the least bit of influence on my personality or conduct. I didn't ask either, not wishing to indulge him in this fancifulness. But from time to time, he has paused at something I have said, some incident or other I have got involved in and nodded wisely, whilst intoning, "Typical Libra." I don't encourage him.

Geoff and I are going to the cinema tonight. It seems an age since I last saw a film at the cinema. Yvonne and I sometimes went. It was usually at her suggestion and it was not usually to see something that might be described as popular cinema. Often there were subtitles, long close-ups. Or it was something in black and white where nothing much seemed to happen. Not that I particularly longed for a tale set in a far-away galaxy, just a good story that keeps you engaged. Cinema-going is one of those things that I have a bit of a psychological barrier about doing alone. Though what is so wrong with that I can't tell, sitting in the dark with strangers instead of with someone else. I had the same inhibition initially about eating out alone. I still wouldn't go to a proper restaurant on my own. The cafe was fine, mass catering, all sorts in and out over the day. I would feel my aloneness, eating by myself in a restaurant. Young people do it more but they are more used to the eating-out culture. It was always an occasion, growing up, a treat, and a rare one at that. You would have looked very conspicuous indeed doing it on your own in those days.

Geoff did mention what we are going to see. He mentioned some actors who are in it and the director. I hadn't heard of any of them. There was a time when I might have done. Cinema was the default 'date' event in a small town, not much else to do, with chips on the way home. You grew up with the pictures; old black and white films on a Sunday afternoon. Saturday morning pictures, which when I was young even showed the odd silent film in the mix of Westerns, serials and worthy, if dull children's films. You got to know familiar faces on the screen, in the films you liked. Everybody went at one time. There were still half a dozen picture houses operating in the town, in my youth. Some became bingo halls as I was growing up, some nightclubs, some carpet showrooms, most were just pulled down. Now it's the big, multi-screen venues, with that deafening stereo sound. But the seating is more comfortable, I have to say.

I am home from the cinema. I had left Zeno at Geoff's house, when we set off so that the dogs would have each other for company, whilst we were out. We called back into Geoff's house and we had a cup of tea, though I thought it was getting a bit late and I might have just got straight off home if Geoff hadn't proposed that I stayed a while. He had a cup of tea too, saying coffee would keep him awake, drinking it this late in the evening.

When we were settled on the sofa, for some reason I suddenly found myself asking about Geoff's partner.

"What was Jim like?" I asked him. "And don't say typical Leo." I knew that was likely how he would start to answer. Geoff laughed.

"Eschewing that area, then," he said, looking thoughtful, "Jim was a bit larger than life, very passionate about everything he valued, about his causes, his work, food. He had large appetites. He had a bit of a temper sometimes, explosive, wore his heart on his sleeve, enthusiastic about things he cared about. All his life he worked very hard, and played very hard at times, lots of energy, restless. He burned bright."

I was trying to imagine this man that Geoff had fallen for. I couldn't guess what he looked like. I can only think how Jim sounded like the polar opposite of me; a ball of energy and enthusiasm. A big personality, probably a big man physically too, hard to encompass.

"I couldn't always keep up with Jim," Geoff continued, "when we first got together there were a lot of rows, arguments. My heart was never in them but he needed an antagonist and I played that part. He calmed down as he grew older. I think I mellowed him out a bit but that intensity still simmered underneath, as a potential. He was, well, in short, he was leonine." After a pause, he added, "Very different to you."

"How so?" I asked. I was a little surprised that Geoff had chosen to make me Jim's comparator, even though I had just mentally characterised myself in relation to Jim as his contrary, just as Geoff did.

"I see you as a bit more buttoned-down, reserved, restrained. Not bad things in themselves. But I don't think that's the whole story with you. I think you might, one day, and perhaps quite soon, let yourself go."

I don't think any of this was meant unkindly. I could even see some of it as complimentary. And I knew what Geoff meant. I had often wondered myself whether I had been too forbearing in my life and if this was really my natural self. I considered then whether Geoff might see this as a fault in me, whether *I* should see it as a fault. Yvonne and I had our moments of raised voices, mainly in the early years. All couples do in that phase, it is part of the process of getting used to each other, getting used to living together and sorting out the parameters of a relationship. As a settled couple, we rarely argued. Little things could annoy

Yvonne, about me mostly. Little things about her annoyed me. But it takes compromise to stick together over a length of time, I believe, give and take. I was never goaded to the point where I lost my temper. If Yvonne did lose it, as she sometimes did, I didn't rise to it. We both had areas of stress in our lives and there are moments when it is good to let off steam. But I was always more laid-back, eager to get things back on a regular footing. A little of the fight went out of Yvonne in time and we had a quieter carry-on.

I have looked back on my marriage a good deal over the past eighteen months. Of late I have become more conscious that in this process I might have occasionally been harsh in my judgements, unfair to Yvonne sometimes. I don't think I was the easiest person to live with. There must have been days when I was sullen and sulky, resentful and uncommunicative. I see those things now, just from being in my own company, let alone how I might have been from time to time living with someone else. I'll never know now her side of this, her perspective. I think I probably wouldn't want to know.

Geoff and I talked about the film we had seen, a little. Geoff had enjoyed it and I think I liked it, though I got a bit lost with the plot at one stage (I could have nodded off briefly). The story was about a boy who goes missing in childhood, presumed kidnapped, presumed murdered or something. He turns up years later, all grown up, with little memory of the intervening years, though his parents and the authorities didn't seem to probe too deeply into where he had been. The thing was, was he who he claimed to be? There were hints at something supernatural going on. It was left a bit unresolved at the end, I think, unless I missed something. Everyone seemed to just decide to ignore the discrepancies in the young man's story, for the sake of having the family back together. The boy's parents, who had divorced after the trauma, were reunited but the mother's face, in a big close-up in the final scene, suggested that there was trouble in store, something not quite right. Maybe the producers were preparing the groundwork for a sequel. But then again, modern films often leave loose ends, not like the black and white days.

As I was leaving Geoff's house, much later than I had realised, out of the blue, he invited me to spend Christmas with him. I hadn't really given Christmas much thought. Christmas was still a few weeks away, though even I had noticed that the town was gearing up for the big day, with its tree, lights and decorations, modest but tasteful. The trailers for Christmas telly and the adverts for food, drink and toys were showing every fifteen minutes. I had let it wash over me really. I had, if I had given it any thought at all, assumed that Geoff would have already made plans. He had family that I knew of but when the suggestion was made, I didn't say no.

After Geoff made his suggestion about Christmas, I began to look forward to it but I had a lingering feeling that maybe he would change his mind, that I hadn't clearly said yes, I would like to come. I ran the conversation through in my head and I wasn't sure whether I had actually, positively accepted his invite. Perhaps he had made the invitation out of politeness and was ready to make other plans. On our walks, he had not mentioned it again until I finally asked him what time I should come around and did he need me to bring anything or do anything. It seemed safest to proceed on the assumption that it was all agreed. Geoff reassured me in his response and said I should come as early as I liked. He would walk Bella first thing so join him in the morning, whenever. He wasn't going to make a big fuss about catering, so no need to bring anything.

It is agreed then. I hope it is a relaxed occasion, quiet. But don't we all have kind of mixed feelings about Christmas? Isn't it, as we grow older, more ordeal than ornament to the year? Or is that just me? I don't think so. When I was working as many people dreaded it as were looking forward to it. I heard people talking about it; colleagues would talk to me about it, sometimes at those frantic office Christmas parties that seem compulsory in every workplace, with too much drinking and far too much inappropriate behaviour. The day after such events, the staff, the ones that actually made it into work, groggy and shame-faced, regretted as much as their hangovers that another day would be wasted, when they could have been planning and buying-in for Christmas Day. The talk was often about who was going to whose house for Christmas, who was going to have to accommodate Mother, or Aunt Rose or Granddad, who was going to stay sober to ferry everyone about. What should they buy the kids, with their expectations ridiculously heightened every year, was it time not to buy for the nieces and nephews, who would just want money and not a gift, and if so how much should they give them and didn't they always still expect to have at least a little something to open on the day? Wasn't it all too much expense and too much pressure for just one day? Could they face the supermarket to stock up and why had they left their Christmas shopping so late. Mostly it was how they were going to pay for it all. Everyone seemed relieved to be back at work after it was all over, back to some sort of normality before the smaller peak of New Year, still daunting, loomed in their path.

Even though Yvonne and I did not have the added complication of children to consider, there still seemed to be difficult choices to be made each year. Sharing our time out equitably, trying to ensure no one ended up upset or neglected. Whilst we were courting, through the college years, we each continued to have our Christmas with our respective families, just carrying on as if the old rules still applied. We didn't even see each other on some of those Christmas Days. There were no buses running, and we really lived just that little bit too far away for me to walk over to Yvonne's parents' place just to say hello, before trudging back. I didn't dare excuse myself for the three hours or so such a journey would have taken out of the family Christmas and it was out of the question that Yvonne should ask her dad to stay sober and run her over to ours, so we could see each other. We got used to just saying Happy Christmas when we separated on Christmas Eve and did not meet up again until the day after Boxing Day. Even a quick phone call seemed problematic to organise at home.

After we were married, considering the Christmases that had gone before whilst we were students, I would have preferred to have our first Christmases just the two of us, making up for all the times we had not been able even to meet, and enjoying each other's company. But this option did not arise, was barely discussed. I think, in families, the women tend to stick together, in the decision making. Daughters cleave to mothers, sons are assimilated into the wife's family, rather than the other way around. That, I think, was how our Christmases were determined, by Yvonne and her mother. We always went over to Yvonne's parents for Christmas, the sister and her family came too. We stayed there through to the New Year, arriving on Christmas Eve; Yvonne's sister just came over on Christmas Day, getting there after lunch and going home in the evening. When we bought our car, I would fit in a visit to my parents on Christmas Day, usually later in the evening, and Yvonne came with me sometimes. My parents spent the day together and by themselves. My sister had moved away so I felt a bit of an obligation to at least see them but it felt a little perfunctory most of the time, tagged on as an after-thought for form's sake when the main event was all but over. I did feel that we failed to give them their due.

It had been their tradition to go out for Christmas lunch. Mother never fancied the big cook on the day itself, so we went to a local hotel, and had since I was about five. Ridiculously expensive for what you got but for them, it was a grand treat, silver service, a huge tree and long frocks. They continued up to when Father died. In later years, they sometimes went for the whole holiday, from Christmas Eve to Boxing Day. They made friends who they only seemed to see at the hotel, over that season. The two years that Mother was a widow, I insisted we host her over Christmas. Whilst we stayed at home, Yvonne's parents went to Yvonne's sister and stayed there for a few days. We once made the trip to join them on Boxing Day but it was a lot of driving in one day and felt like a bit of a burden on the sister.

The few years we were together in Cornubay, we had Christmas just the two of us. Her sister came over on Boxing Day but the husband never bothered. The boys came with her the first year but after that, they were old enough to make their own decisions. We opened the presents and had a sherry. I went out for a walk with Zeno, taking the boys the year they came, to allow Yvonne to have some time alone with her sister. We had a bit of tea and Christmas cake and Yvonne's sister went home. It was not much of an event. Each of the clubs and groups Yvonne was part of seemed to have some sort of celebration in the lead up to Christmas, so her party frock got a good airing. I was sort of invited to the odd event but not encouraged to attend. I didn't know the people and Zeno would be on her own, so I was happy to decline. She usually came home a bit merry, sometimes a bit too worse for wear for my taste. Yvonne enjoyed a party, whereas I am not comfortable in large gatherings.

Christmas Day itself was always quiet. Yvonne would be out on Christmas Eve and usually did not get up until late morning. By then, I had walked Zeno and done a bit of preparation for lunch. We still had a turkey but few of the trimmings. Zeno would be eating turkey for a week. Most of what we had when we moved here was shop-bought. Once of a day, Yvonne would bake a few mince pies and I even tried my hand at Christmas cake and Christmas pudding now and again. Latterly, we just did a big shop for what was needed. I hadn't realised till then how you could buy stuffing, roasties and Yorkshire puddings that just needed to be heated up. We tried to just buy in what we would get through in a day (With maybe something cold for Boxing Day) but there was always too much. What with the food and the decorations around the house, that looked more and more threadbare with each passing year, partly I wondered why we bothered. But it's a tradition, I suppose, and I didn't want to be the one to say, let's not make a fuss this year, let's not bother with the tree and tinsel, it's just the two of us.

On my own, I have treated Christmas Day almost like any other day. The first one without Yvonne, with her only gone a matter of months, I felt so miserable I only got out of bed to walk Zeno. The half-empty brandy bottle in the larder looked very tempting but it would have been cowardly and demoralising to give in. I sent no cards that year. Few came for me, in any case. Yvonne got more. After that first Christmas, I did make more of an effort but I had put the decorations out with the rubbish. I wasn't going to bother with those again. I cooked lunch. Not a turkey but something I could share with Zeno, with no leftovers anticipated. The community centre puts on a free Christmas lunch on the day, for the old folk, for those on their own, for those without the means. Volunteers staff it. Donations fund it. I can just imagine it. It's not for me.

Thinking about how Christmas will be this year, I don't want to load it with promise or too much expectation. It is not about the past, how things were, good or bad. I want to go beyond any negative thoughts. I think I am distant enough now, have seen the season come and go a sufficient number of times, with just me and Zeno, to be more of a blank page, not unduly engaged with what is whirling about me. Geoff isn't the kind of person to sign up to conventional assumptions of how things should be anyway. I hope I can just relax and enjoy myself. And not drink too much.

It is late, after eleven o'clock, on Christmas night and I have arrived back home from spending the day with Geoff. I didn't feel quite ready yet for bed. I have put the telly on and there is some Christmas special on, a comedy show, a repeat of something shown last year. I am barely watching it but I feel the need to sit up a bit, to unwind and reflect a little before bed. Initially, Zeno jumped up beside me on the sofa and snuggled in but soon she retired to her crate, to sleep properly. She looked very tired. She is snoring quietly now.

It was a different type of Christmas today. I have a sneaking fear that it has reminded me of the day out that Geoff and I spent in Cornubay when we decided to enjoy it as holidaymakers might. I worry that I experienced Christmas as an event in the same way, almost again as a tourist. That I did not engage with it as a celebrant, giving myself wholeheartedly to the traditions and trappings but more as an observer posing as a participant.

I have always felt a bit of an outsider to the festivities, after childhood at least, like they weren't meant for me, like they were what other people did. I subscribed to the view that it was really for the children, for families, all the malarky. Now I wonder if my day was tinged with a bit of irony.

I keep mulling this over but it is getting me nowhere.

Perhaps the day was as genuinely enjoyable as I think it was and I'm just adding complications and, as I always do, not letting myself join in, let go and have fun. It's a bit hard to explain. I should have just gone straight to bed.

But what am I saying really? The truth surely is that I had a lovely day, spent in good company and good cheer. What more could be asked?

Going over to Geoff's earlier this Christmas morning, the town seemed very quiet. You half expect the streets to be thronged with children, trying out the new bikes or whatever, that they have just received from Father Christmas. But you remember then that the town is largely a retirement home at this time of year and the families that do live here are usually further out of town, away from the front, in the newer estates. I noticed that there were church bells ringing, distantly. The day was quite mild, with no sign of snow, a pale sun. All was calm, all was bright. I couldn't hear the sea. The tide must have been a long way out and pacified for the day. No one passed me as I walked, and there were few cars on the roads. Lights twinkled on Christmas trees in the front windows of houses along the way. It was still quite early, I realised.

Geoff greeted me warmly when I arrived before quickly disappearing into the kitchen. I took off my coat and detached Zeno's lead. For some reason, Geoff had seemed a little reluctant for her to come but I couldn't leave her all day alone, I didn't want to leave her, and I didn't want to pop back halfway through the day to let her out. Bella said hello to Zeno with the usual ceremonies. Left to myself, I drifted into the sitting room and began to browse. On a small table near the fireplace, I spotted a framed photograph of a man I assumed must be Jim. I had not noticed it before so perhaps Geoff had put it on display recently, almost in pride of place, as if to include Jim in the festive time. This struck me as a touching gesture. I was reluctant to pick the photograph up but I certainly stopped to have a closer look. I guessed that this was Jim in his early forties, so taken some while ago. Perhaps this was how Geoff best remembered him, conceivably this was near the start of their relationship. It could have been Cornubay in the background or somewhere local at least. It was a coastal setting, Jim on a beach, a definite breeze discernible and majestic waves breaking behind him. Jim was squinting into the sun, smiling broadly. He was a burly chap, as I somehow suspected, rugby build I think some call it, bearded. I couldn't say whether he was handsome or not, that was up to Geoff but he looked a pleasant sort of person, friendly. Geoff came into the room and saw me looking at the photograph but he didn't say anything.

Whatever Geoff was cooking seemed to require regular visits to the kitchen and in one of his absences, I looked at his bookshelves. Geoff has quite a few books. The stock in the sitting room was mainly novels, some reference books, a shelf of non-fiction, biography, and stuff about film. No particular order that I could see, definitely not alphabetical. One section of the bookcase stood out, five or six books together, all about fish or the coast, all with Dr James Connor as author or co-author. It took me a few moments to work out that these must have been written by Geoff's partner. One, written with another chap, photographs by someone else, was a big, glossy book, a guide to rock pools. It looked interesting and I took it down.

"You've found Jim's archive," said Geoff, now standing behind me, "most are pretty dry. Academic stuff. That one that you have was aimed at a more popular market and it sold quite well. There was talk at one point of a television series but it didn't come to anything. It still sells a few copies each year."

I was impressed by this. Geoff said I could borrow it if I wanted to but I didn't bother at that stage.

Thankfully, Geoff had not gone over the top with the Christmas thing. There was a small tree, with lights but it looked as if it came straight out of the box each year, ready to plug in. He had received more cards than I had but I resisted the temptation to browse them to see who they were from. He was cooking salmon for lunch. He was not one for roasts. He had told me not long before that he had considered giving up meat altogether, particularly the processed kind. It was only due to the fact that he would have had to give up our Tuesdays that he continued to eat bacon and sausage, he said. I wasn't sure I entirely believed this. He seemed to love his bacon when it was served very crispy.

We had sherry before lunch. It seemed traditional; a bit on the dry side for my taste.

I was a little disconcerted to find that Geoff had bought me presents. He had even got something for Zeno, which seemed a bit daft to me (I never understood that). I felt somewhat mortified that I hadn't even thought about buying him anything. In view of the last time I had attempted it, I hadn't considered bringing wine. Geoff was much more of a connoisseur than me in these matters so I had left it to him. To not be totally empty-handed, I had brought a Christmas cactus for Geoff and a box of after-dinner mints, posh ones, so I hoped this was enough to fulfil social obligations.

Geoff's presents were very neatly wrapped, a skill I had never quite acquired. I think women are naturally more adept at present wrapping than men. But Geoff had cracked it. It looked like a quite expensive wrapping paper too; quite thick, subtly decorated, nothing kitsch or glittery. It was a shame to open them but Geoff encouraged me, and in the order he handed them to me.

There were a couple of the more jokey things that people buy these days for these occasions. There was a candy breakfast (They have them in the little beachside shops here), bacon, eggs and sausage made out of the rock, I suppose. I hoped he didn't expect me to eat it. I suspected it had been on the shelf in the shop for years. But it was a nice thought, referencing how we had first become acquainted I suppose. He gave me a mug with a picture of Zeno on it. I know there are online places where these things can be created cheaply. I could not imagine when he had photographed Zeno. It was not something I had noticed him doing but then again there must have been many opportunities. It looked like she was on the beach. I would find a place for it.

Finally, Geoff had got me a book about Zeno. I don't mean the dog but the man. I have always resisted learning about Zeno the man. I must have told Geoff this. On first glance, I saw references on the cover to Zeno's 'paradoxes'. It's a bit of a paradox to me that Geoff bought this for me. Geoff said something cryptic, when I held the book in my hand, about how paradoxes can sometimes illuminate rather obscure a subject, that I would find Zeno's ideas interesting and that the fact that he and my dog shared a name didn't diminish or limit either of them. He is right, of course. Now that I know at least who the chap is and his line of business, as it were, I find it doesn't impact how I feel about my Zeno. Not one bit. I might try and read the book, for Geoff's sake. I am sure he will ask me at some point what I think about it. But I don't think philosophy is really in my line. Still, I thought all of the presents represented a nice gesture and clearly something that he had put some thought and effort into. I thanked him, whilst of course saying that he shouldn't have.

Lunch was very palatable, not too heavy, really quite delicate. I liked the salmon. It's not a fish I have partaken of much, except in my youth, when it came out of a tin and was considered quite a treat when served with lettuce, cucumber and tomato on a Sunday afternoon. This fish still had its skin on, with the odd bone here and there but it went down well, with a sauce, with lots of herbs, which was quite sharp. Pudding was ice cream, made by Geoff, with a Christmas pudding flavour. At least it honoured the season in that respect and was eatable.

After lunch, we continued to pay homage to the Christmas traditions, eating too many chocolates, drinking too many beers and sampling some of those liqueurs and other drinks that surely no one ever goes near apart from at Christmas (Advocaat, for goodness' sake). We watched an old film that both of us had seen many times, before tuning in to the Queen's speech. We reminisced about our childhood Christmases and our favourite ever Christmas presents. Predictably, we both opted for a bike. We talked about how we had spent Christmas with our partners and how we had managed after their deaths (Geoff had spent his with family, though he would have preferred to be alone). That discussion did not bring the mood down in any way. It felt right to celebrate those times and those people. Every Christmas seems to me to be as much about

Christmases past as about Christmas present. It is always an occasion when memory and the moment coalesce. Whatever memories we have, and no matter over what period they have accumulated, there will always be something linked to loss, something partaking of regret, about them.

"I think I knew your wife, by sight," Geoff said after we had looked back at old times together. I knew that on a couple of occasions Geoff had studied the photographs of Yvonne that are around my house. No doubt he had made some connection. "She was a striking woman."

That was not an adjective that had been applied to Yvonne before that I recalled, certainly not by me. I could see his point, I suppose. Yvonne had noticeable red hair, needing a little assistance in later life to keep its lustre but she maintained the colour to the end, a hair appointment every week. She was quite tall for a woman, always well turned out, never went out without her face on, as she put it.

"Jim and I liked to patronise the amateur theatre productions at the Winter Gardens. I recall her being in a couple of their productions. She did draw the eye, even though she didn't have any large roles in anything that we saw. I used to see her in the library quite a bit too."

"We usually went to the library together," I said.

"Really? Well, I must have missed you. I don't recall ever serving you. Plus the library is often used as a rendezvous point for people. It's very central and a good place to meet up with friends, especially on wet days. I think that at least half the people in the library at any given time are there for social reasons rather than to borrow a book. Some people come in every day, read the paper, chat with friends. We were never too strict about maintaining silence as some libraries are. The librarians chat to customers as much as anyone."

As Geoff talked about coming across Yvonne, it struck me how all our lives criss-cross weekly and daily. We are largely unaware of these intersections, until that point where the passing and re-passing becomes a sort of collision. When some spur or catalyst causes us to notice someone or something, like that first breakfast with Geoff, I suppose. They have been there all along, their lives and our own trundling along parallel paths. Adjacent lives we are never consciously aware of until suddenly we are. Something arrests us in our progress, it may be momentary and we walk on; it may lead us somewhere we never imagined. Is there a kind of fate in this, I wondered, or just a random interplay of forces? I have lived a lot of my life, I suspect most of us have lived our lives, not noticing, just letting the parade pass on, without deep thought, inattentive and uninvolved.

Apart from Yvonne, and some friends at school and university, Geoff is one of the few people I have got to know on a one-to-one basis. There were work colleagues I got to know well over a period of years, people with whom I developed a rapport or shared a bit of banter but it never transferred out of work and more or less ended there. I didn't keep in touch with anyone from work after I retired. Those relationships were only sustained in that specific context and environment. They couldn't be transplanted. I didn't want them to be. Of course, when I was working there was some socialising outside work but that was always in a group. The idea of sharing confidences or getting to know someone on a personal level just did not arise. I think when people have children that makes more of a common bond between them. People at work didn't talk to me much about their children, so important in their lives and absent from mine. But then, I didn't ask them about their children. Maybe I never asked the right questions, never showed an appropriate level of interest. I think I got on with most people, had a degree of respect from them. I consciously avoided making favourites but it might also be true that I set limits that I barely recognised as to how close people could approach me, boundaries anyone would be reluctant to cross. I probably thought Yvonne was too open with other people. Maybe the truth is that I was too closed off.

By teatime, we were neither of us in the mood for more food but we fed the dogs and took them out on a short walk around the town. It was dark by then and we cut down the high street, to look at the lights. Not a soul was about. The sound of the sea suggested a swell gathering, way out beyond the lights. We were not out for long and we were both looking forward to getting back into the warmth. Geoff had left his curtains open and his little tree glowed in the half-light. At that moment, everything felt right. Nothing strange or wrongly placed.

Geoff had baked some mince pies and we ate one or two of these when we returned. I had a cup of tea before we went back to beer but we made one beer last for the rest of the evening. We settled down to watch another hour or so of television again. There wasn't anything, in particular, we wanted to watch. I think it was a Christmas-themed, nostalgic murder mystery but it didn't hold my attention and in keeping with the spirit of the day, we both found ourselves dozing off as the evening drew in. I was the first to awake and watched Geoff for a while as he slept on. Zeno had squeezed in beside me, as I had slept. I was alert to the novelty of our situation as I looked around me. A year before, I could never have imagined being there, in that company, on that day.

I stayed at Geoff's house later than I had intended when I had set out this morning. I have been home for more than a couple of hours now and it is well past midnight. The heating went off some time ago and I am beginning to feel the chill. I'm tired. I should go to bed.

After enjoying the Christmas break with Geoff, I was a bit hopeful that we might see in the New Year together. Geoff did not mention this, however, and I was a bit reluctant to make this suggestion myself. I don't why I have this inhibition about taking the initiative, why I wait to be asked, rather than doing the asking. This morning, when I met Geoff at our usual spot and we set off to walk the dogs together, Geoff explained what his plans were. He was going to see his mother and his sister.

"Not something I am looking forward to, particularly," said Geoff.

Geoff's mother is still alive, he told me, past ninety but in relatively good physical health but her mind was going. Up until about a year ago, she was still living at home, coping more or less, and supported by Geoff's younger sister, who lived nearby. Around Christmas time the previous year, it had become clear that she could not manage on her own any longer. Geoff's sister had probably felt this for some time but had only raised it with Geoff then. His mother had gone into respite care over the Christmas holiday and had never returned home. Geoff intended to go back to his hometown, to meet with his family to review the position with his mother. It would be a melancholy visit but one that was necessary. He would stay with his sister for a couple of days. He would let me know when he was back in circulation.

I was not too concerned about spending the New Year alone. It was how it had been for a few years now and I was used to it. Yvonne and I had no traditions about it. After our family responsibilities ended, we never really celebrated New Year or marked it in a special way. We stayed at home and tended to go to bed at our usual times. We might have had a couple of quiet drinks but Yvonne never wanted to go out, with her friends or with me, despite the invitations she, we, received. I was relieved about this. I found the whole occasion forced and frantic, not to mention a waste of money. The hike in prices in bars and restaurants for New Year celebrations always irked me.

Yvonne herself was always a bit maudlin about this time of year. I caught a bit of that emotion from her. I can see why. The date obliged you to think about another year gone by, another year closer to the grave. Why celebrate when all you had to look forward to was ageing, decay and snow. If anything, it feels to me that the New Year begins around April, when the world is back in bud. The weather always seems to turn for the worst as soon as New Year's Day has passed, colder, bleaker. It does not have the character to encourage you to think of a fresh start, to view the world with optimism.

Though I never saw the need or the point of it, Yvonne did like to go in for New Year resolutions, usually around eating and drinking and exercise. Needless to say, these good intentions didn't usually survive the week. She always did seem a bit brighter once the second of January arrived; things starting up again, the shops opening, friends contacting her to arrange things.

New Year does not bother me now, being on my own. I'm happy to be at home by the fire, watching a bit of telly, feeling no obligations whatsoever to the season. It doesn't bring back memories, any that I want to revive anyway. It doesn't prompt me to look back or look forward. Other dates in the calendar matter more to me. It's the fag-end of the festive celebrations. People invest too much in it. When I worked, I was just glad that my head would be clear and things would get back to normal, the day after New Year, all the nonsense packed away with the Christmas decorations, for another year.

I still stay up past midnight on New Year's Eve because of the fireworks, which I don't remember being a feature of local celebrations until the millennium. Zeno is sometimes bothered by the noise of them, so I linger until they are over with in case she needs a bit of comfort. Often she just sleeps through them, and so do I.

Going into this New Year, I do feel I am approaching the future with more anticipation and serenity than I have for some time. I have made a life of my own in a sense, begun to find my own way of doing things, arranging things, pastimes, such as they are. I still miss Yvonne but wounds heal over time and time has passed. There does feel to be something different, something new in my life, things to look forward to, not just the year turning on its axis. On New Year's Day, I will take Zeno out early. It will be quieter than usual. Geoff suggested he might ring me, whilst he was away. I didn't discourage him.

We have begun the New Year now. There is snow in the air. The sea was choppy when Zeno and I took our walk; a cold breeze off the sea. The town was deserted, shops all closed, even the corner shop. It was still dark enough to make me think I had made a mistake about the time and left a few hours earlier than I had intended. Zeno shivered a bit and looked miserable. She doesn't like this time of year. My feet were cold. Zeno did what she had to do as soon as we were on a grassy bit, before we even got to the beach. I don't think either of us was good company at that point. I realised, on days like this, that if I wasn't careful Zeno could easily become a fair-weather dog and me a fair-weather dog-walker.

The phone was ringing as I entered the house. It seemed early for a call. I didn't reach the house phone in time but then my mobile phone began to ring. I had a slight apprehension about bad news, though who would have urgent news for me I couldn't guess. It turned out to be Geoff calling me, wishing me a happy new year. He told me that he was already packed and ready to come home. His mother was worse, did not know him now, had lost weight and seemed in a rapid decline. His sister had rowed with her husband almost as soon as Geoff had arrived and there was an atmosphere in the house throughout his stay. Geoff wondered if he was not really welcome. His nephew had come home drunk at two in the morning on New Year's Day and had been sick in the hall. Another row had ensued. Geoff had not slept well and missed home and our morning walk. Bella hadn't settled and Geoff had found it difficult to soothe her whining in the nights. He was ready to come back, though he had planned to stay a few more days. There did not seem to be any point and he didn't think his presence was helping his sister and her family reconcile their differences. He would be on his way as soon as he put the phone down.

Geoff had said that whilst he experienced his sleepless nights, he had browsed the local listings and found a play that was running nearby that looked interesting. He thought we should go, for a change, for a treat. I said he should pop around when he got back and we could have a chat about it and make the arrangements.

Last night, Geoff and I had our trip to the theatre.

Something happened.

I am still not entirely sure what to make of it. A year ago, I would have known exactly how to feel about it, where I would place it in the scheme of my thoughts, experience and emotions. I would have had a clear and unequivocal reaction but now I am at a loss. I am in an unfamiliar landscape with only a vague idea as to how I got here and no concept of my ultimate destination or even my next few steps.

I had arrived early at Geoff's house. At his suggestion, I had brought Zeno with me. We would be out of the house for a good few hours; the drive to the theatre itself was about half an hour. The dogs would be fine, I thought. Zeno generally slept most of the evening after her walk. But Geoff thought they would be company for each other and I agreed with him. The weather had become colder, icy and we talked about the state of the roads for the journey. Neither of us made the suggestion that we should not go but we should make the journey carefully. Geoff would drive.

I had only come a little way into the living room. I had kept my coat on, thinking it might be best not to get too comfortable and that we should probably set off earlier than we planned and allow plenty of time for the drive. We could always have a drink at the bar if we arrived too early. We let the dogs out into the garden for a minute or two, just in case, but I don't think they were out long enough to do anything. They would settle down together, I knew. Geoff put his coat on and turned to face me. He tucked my scarf in, a little closer to my neck, he reached his hands up towards me.

Then Geoff kissed me.

It was not a deep, penetrating kiss, just a soft pressing of his lips to mine.

I found I was not horrified.

Rather than being shocked or even faintly disgusted, as I thought I should have been in the abstract, I found instead, as it was happening in reality, that I was completely focused on the physical sensations; the nearness of him; that he was slightly shorter than me, so I must have leaned down a little to meet him or he stretched up; the warmth of his hand on the back of my neck. I felt the gentleness of his movements. They were tentative enough to require that each element of the gesture had to be wholly with my consent or it would have been arrested or abandoned by him, at any point. It was almost as if I participated with a sense of curiosity rather than surrender. But I did not pull away, I gravitated forward. My response was reciprocal, complementary but not anticipatory. It seemed so long since I had last been kissed by anyone, that I had somewhat forgotten how it felt or how to feel about it, almost as if I was being kissed for the first time. It was the first time, really.

So, if I was pressed and had to say, one way or another, did I enjoy it, I honestly would have to say, I don't know. It was certainly not unpleasant. I had no urge to run away afterwards or to be outraged or offended. It felt appropriate, even inevitable, in the context.

The thing that surprised me, if anything, was stubble. Geoff is fair-haired or once was; now he has as much grey as fair. Either way, his beard is not very noticeable, even after a day or so of growth. I had not imagined that in the closeness of a kiss, it would chafe a little. I wondered how women put up with it. I had noticed, I suppose, that slight rash or redness that some women sometimes referred to as stubble burn. I had not thought about it. I like a close shave myself, every day, sometimes twice a day, but even so on rare occasions, I did recall Yvonne pulling away and wincing a little, saying, ouch, stubble, as we kissed. I did not realise, till Geoff kissed me that the close contact involved in being kissed by a man can feel like a quick rasp with sandpaper. I know, as we separated, that my hand went instinctively to my chin as if I was puzzling over what had just occurred, as if I had been branded in a subtle way that I needed to reflect on.

Geoff left his hand resting on my shoulder and did not move completely away.

"Was that all right?" he asked, looking into my eyes, to read my thoughts.

I nodded slowly. I thought he might do it again. I thought perhaps I wanted him to do it again as if that might clarify my feelings about it. He stood, gazing at me a little longer, then squeezed my shoulder and stepped back.

"We should get going, I suppose," he said.

As I did not immediately respond to Geoff but stood stock-still where he had left me, he added, "You do still want to go?"

"Of course," I said, coming back to myself.

Did he wonder that the kiss had changed things, spoilt things maybe? That I wanted to run away, never see him again? From my perspective, without the opportunity to give it any deep thought at that moment, I felt that it had changed nothing. Or if it had changed things, it was not inevitably in a bad way.

I stepped outside and waited for Geoff as he locked up. He smiled at me and we crossed to the drive, got into his car and drove off.

The local roads were still a bit slippery and Geoff drove carefully until we made it to the main road out of town, where grit had been scattered and it was easier to make progress. The heater in the car soon warmed up. I looked across at Geoff, as he concentrated on the road until he looked back at me.

The play was entertaining enough: at least it held my attention for most of the time. Despite her own theatrical interests and ambitions or maybe because of them, Yvonne and I were never regular playgoers, usually no more than once a year. I saw Yvonne on stage those few times and we had been very occasionally to the theatre in London and, more often, locally. We never went after we moved here. I wonder if Yvonne had some degree of envy about 'professionals', as she called them, with a twist in her voice. Maybe she was reluctant to seek comparisons with her own stage performances. If we did go to the theatre it always seemed to be to something a bit obscure, ambiguous, experimental or foreign or all of them combined. Something totally out of her line of theatrics and something that I had no framework within which to judge it. The plays never featured actors I had heard of or seen on the television. It was often something in a tiny theatre or a room over a pub. How she found them, I don't know. Sometimes there was someone she was friendly with in the play. Sometimes she vaguely knew the author or the director. Yvonne seemed to enjoy the plays. I was generally a bit baffled. There always seemed to be a lot of nudity in them too. I mean, where are you supposed to look?

The play that Geoff and I saw was more accessible. Something about a divorcing couple and a comic mix-up about a person (Gender unspecified) who it appeared was having an affair with both the husband and the wife, unbeknownst to either party. It was touching at times, a bit silly at others. Technically, I think it was billed as a comedy or perhaps a farce. If there was a message behind the antics, it might have been that honesty is the best policy and that accommodation is always possible if all the facts are disclosed and approached in a grown-up way. Whether Geoff had a message for me in his choice of the play, I couldn't be sure.

I suppose I deferred my reaction to Geoff's kiss and put it from my head whilst we were out. I am still leaving the whole episode in a kind of mental box. Geoff did not allude to it, directly or indirectly, for the rest of that evening. We talked about the play on the way back. I was still sort of thinking that I should feel that my world had shifted but I was in a kind of delayed shock. It was an odd situation, as if I was not myself, despite part of me sensing that I was more myself than I had ever been or that the self I thought I knew had dimensions I had not guessed at. When I get to this point in my thinking, I keep putting the matter aside as too complicated, even now.

When we got back to Geoff's house, Zeno did not rush to greet me, as she usually does when I come back to our house, from shopping, or wherever. Perhaps she was still not familiar enough with the layout of Geoff's house or the sounds of the house, to recognise when someone entered. As we went in, we saw Bella and Zeno nestled together on the couch, very cosy and fast asleep. They looked very sweet together. Geoff and I both paused to look at them. Eventually, they stirred and Zeno gave me a little tail wag without actually getting up off the sofa to greet me.

"They seem very settled," said Geoff, "seems almost a pity to disturb them."
I smiled.

"You could stay here tonight if you wanted to," said Geoff. He waited, before adding, "The spare bed is made up."

Cold as the night was, cosy as Zeno looked, and reluctant as I was to face even the short walk back home and an empty house, I judged it best to go. I said this to Geoff and I roused Zeno. She came willingly enough. Bella and Geoff followed us to the door and saw us off.

I have been up for a while now; drinking tea and thinking my random thoughts, watching the skies get light. In a few moments, I will have to stir myself and Zeno to meet Geoff and Bella for our morning walk. That is part of my routine now.

It still looks a bit icy underfoot, so maybe a shorter walk will be in order, keeping to the main roads. I am sure that my thoughts will clear after a brisk walk and an hour or so in Geoff's company.

At breakfast this morning Geoff said that he had been reflecting on his mother and her condition when he last saw her. There was not the remotest chance of her returning to her home now. Geoff's sister had done enough, more so than Geoff, who had begun to think that he should have got more involved and sooner. He had spoken to his sister the previous evening and they had come to the conclusion that his mother's house should be sold to pay for her continuing care. His sister had already set all the legal requirements in place to empower them to do this. The house had now stood more or less empty for a year and it seemed best to conclude the matter before it deteriorated any further or it became a target for vandalism or a break-in. The neighbours had kept an eye on it but the situation had to be remedied.

Geoff said he intended to go back to his hometown for a spell to meet with his sister, see his mother and begin the arrangements for the sale of the house and its clearance. This time he would stay in his mother's house, rather than with his sister. It would give the house an airing and he would be on site to make a start on packing things up and disposing of them. Geoff's mother had never really sorted the house out after his father died; many of his father's possessions and clothes were still there. It could take a while to tackle what needed to be done.

I commiserated with Geoff. I know how daunting this task can be. Geoff did not say anything else immediately and sat watching me.

"I don't know how long I will be gone," Geoff said.

I wasn't sure what more to say.

"There is quite a bit of work to do," he continued, "I'd rather not go but it has to be done."

We seemed to be feeling our way clumsily towards a conclusion.

"What will you do with yourself, whilst I'm gone?"

I shrugged. "Just carry on as normal, I suppose. Walk Zeno. Potter about."

Geoff nodded and waited.

I felt that the onus was now on me to say something, initiate something for a change, or lose something if I was not careful.

"Would you like me to come with you?" I said. "I could give you a hand with everything."

This was certainly what Geoff hoped to hear from me. In the end, it had been quite easy for me to make this suggestion. It somehow had to come from me. I think we both knew that I would have likely said no if Geoff had made the proposal.

"Yes, please," said Geoff, relieved and pleased, "it would be a great help and good to have some company. I wish we could make it a sort of holiday but there will be some sad duties for me. I hope we can see a bit of the place, though, and I would like you to meet my sister and her family."

So that is resolved. We depart tomorrow. I need to pack.

We have been in Geoff's parents' house for two days now.

We took Geoff's car when we drove over to his hometown. Geoff was not sure how long we would be staying, how long the job would take or at least how long he would be able to endure it. He did not have a clear idea of what would be required, what difficulties, legal and so on, might arise and what memories might be stirred. I did consider driving over there in my own car. There was a brief moment of what I think was a form of claustrophobia when I mulled over the coming stay at the house. What if we did not get on? What if Zeno could not settle? What if I missed my own place and all its familiar things? What if I just got bored with it all? In just the one car, Geoff's car, I would not have an easy escape route. Either Geoff would have to drive me back or I would have to catch a train or something. The whole situation could become awkward. It was hard for me to stop these thoughts from filtering through my head. It was unknown territory. In the end, I saw the sense in us all crowding into the one car, with the dogs. We both probably packed too much stuff and it was a squeeze.

The house was a bungalow. Not Geoff's childhood home but a place his parents had bought as a retirement home. It was clear that there had been some years of neglect and a period when the home had not been lived in. There was a slight smell of damp, a little mould in the kitchen and bathroom. It felt cold and bereft. Geoff had brought clean sheets and we made up the beds in the two bedrooms, tucking hot water bottles into each of them, to give the bedclothes an airing. Geoff turned the heating on and opened a couple of windows. There was a garden, not enclosed completely, so we kept an eye on Zeno and Bella when we let them out to get used to their new surroundings. Geoff lit the gas fire too and put the kettle on.

There was clearly quite a bit of sorting to do. Shelves were solidly packed with knick-knacks, photographs and ornaments, layered with dust, pictures lined the walls. Cupboards were overflowing and there was barely space on any kitchen surface to put down a cup. Every room was overcrowded with furniture.

I gathered that some downsizing had taken place when his parents had moved here but there was still the accumulated clutter of a lifetime to tackle. Yvonne and I had gone through a similar process when we moved to Cornubay. There is nothing like moving house, when you see your home packed in innumerable boxes, to make you acutely aware of the level of your accumulation. I think that I disposed of more stuff than Yvonne but we did get rid of some furniture, books, CDs, crockery and a few other bits and pieces. A fraction of what we could have discarded. We all hang on to too much. Things we will never look at again, wear again, use again, we still cling to. There must be boxes of stuff I could still chuck out. Perhaps, as we age, we all build these walls, these barricades of stuff around us. Thankfully, there was no garage at the bungalow, the traditional home for life's useless accretions.

Geoff began his task almost as soon as we arrived. I helped him make up a few boxes to pack things up, things for the charity shop, things for the tip but I concluded that there was not much more I could do after that. I helped him take clothes off hangers but this quickly began to feel too personal and reminded me too much of Yvonne, that lingering scent of old perfume and dust. I had no idea what, from this other, unknown life, this separate past of Geoff and his family, was worth preserving. Not much, it seemed, as I watched Geoff throwing swathes of clothes, papers and books about, filling bag after bag, as if in a rush to dispose of the past. He paused occasionally over certain items, before he disposed of them or set them aside, so there must have been some system to his activities. I saw him linger a while over a small ornament, a tiny green vase, with a kind of gilding to it. Old, it looked. I wondered what associations it held for him. He put it back on the shelf where he had found it and carried on.

I know from experience of this task that every drawer you open, every item you turn over in your hands, has its own little splinter of memory attached to it. You can avoid it by taking handfuls of the stuff and just dumping it, unfiltered into the charity box. Or you can spend half a day on a small corner of a cupboard, drifting off into a fog of recollection. Geoff seemed to be in a hurry but even he could not help but pause now and then.

I kept Geoff company in his tidying for a while, sealing up boxes as he filled them but I couldn't help him decide what to keep and what to discard. In the end, I wandered off to do a bit of shopping for our dinner. I think the task was stirring up old memories for both of us and reminded me that I had only half-completed the task to clearing out Yvonne's stuff. I had not had the strength or the will at the time to finish the job. I began to feel I should continue my own duties of sifting and disposing of things once we were back home.

The next day, for a break from the clearing out, Geoff took me on a tour of his hometown, though it didn't take long. After we set off, it seemed like he had had second thoughts about the tour, as if he was not sure he wanted to revisit his past, as if he suddenly found the memories oppressive. He had not lived in the town since the day he left for university, even avoiding coming back during vacations if he could. Geoff was less forthcoming than I had ever known him when I asked him even quite trivial questions about the town and the places he showed me. From what were no more than hints and generalities, I put together a picture of his home life and history with the place.

Geoff showed me his childhood home where he had lived from birth to university. It could have been anywhere, a terraced house in any town. It looked like the area had seen better days but Geoff did not say whether this had always been the case or the neglect had happened after he had left home. Geoff barely paused as he gave a vague indication as to the particular house that was his home. I couldn't tell you now which it was. I am not sure I could even identify the street. He didn't say anything as we drove by, even shrugging off the few questions I asked him. I don't think I saw Geoff at any point look directly at the house that had been his old home.

We passed, very quickly it seemed to me, his old schools and some local features; the pub where he had spent time, drinking underage, a deserted children's playground, the church that he went to as a child. We paused a little near what looked like just waste ground to me but Geoff explained it had been a football pitch once. From the little that Geoff said, there was some sort of grace and some sort of disgrace associated with the place for him.

What the connection between all the places was, whether there was a narrative linking everything together and whether some areas or venues had a more special significance than others, I didn't really discover. I found myself craning my neck to catch a view of some place or other that Geoff briefly pointed out before whisking us away. Nowhere did we actually stop, park and get out of the car to explore.

Geoff's story, from what I discovered of it, I suppose I might have predicted, from the kind of town it was and the kind of person that Geoff was. His father had disapproved of his lifestyle choices, the way he looked and acted, the people he spent time with. Something of a fissure opened up between them as Geoff hit his teens and he was not much in their lives once he had left home. Geoff alluded to bullying at school, a familiar story. But he also spoke of one sympathetic member of staff who had helped Geoff and probably kept him stable enough to do well at school and escape to university. Geoff kept some contact with his mother throughout this time and was always close to his sister. There appeared to have been a fledgling reconciliation with his father, not long before his father was taken ill with the condition that eventually finished him off.

I did not get any strong emotions of anger or even sadness from Geoff when discussing his youth. It seemed to be just stuff that had happened, was long gone and pointless to dwell on or rake over. But I don't think that he had quite the perspective he thought he had about his past when he proposed the tour of his hometown. I think he quickly realised that he had been wrong to think that he could undertake it, reveal to another person the landmarks from his childhood and youth, as if nothing had happened in this town, as if nothing had marked him. He might think that all this did not impinge on him anymore. But when back in the midst of it he could not contain it that easily. He could not encapsulate it as just the place where he had grown up, a kind of anyplace where anyone could have grown to manhood.

Geoff introduced me to his sister yesterday. Geoff had set off early to pick her up, to take her with him to see their mother. The plan was then that his sister would come back to the bungalow to help sort out a few things. I had made myself scarce before she arrived, taking both the dogs out with me for a long walk, to give Geoff and his sister a bit of undisturbed time and space to tackle what needed to be done. I stayed out as long as I could but Bella doesn't have the same stamina as Zeno and I could see her flagging. I guessed Eleanor (He calls her Ellie) would still be there when we arrived back.

She is younger than Geoff, similar in colouring to him, attractive, friendly enough. Geoff and Ellie were filling boxes, looking a bit dusty. I could tell that they got on well together. There was a lot of laughter as I entered the house. Bella liked her too.

Geoff introduced us and we shook hands.

"I've been looking forward to meeting you," she said, "Geoff's new friend."

Was there a special emphasis on that word 'friend' or was that in my imagination? I asked how things were going with the packing. Some progress had been made, if only in terms of decisions about what was to be thrown out. Ellie had made up a small box of items she was going to take home with her. I left them to it but Ellie did not stay much longer after I was back in the house. It was getting close to mealtime. She said she was pleased to meet me and hoped to see more of me. I think I said the right things back in reply. It wasn't the ordeal I had half expected, meeting someone from Geoff's family. So much for all that, I thought afterwards.

We took things more easy, after Ellie had gone. We restacked the boxes to make things look neater and to make it easier to assess what still needed to be done. Geoff made a quick trip to the charity shop and I cleaned up here and there before putting the tea on. It felt like we had reached the end of a phase in the process. We watched television in the evening. The settings on the TV set had been cranked up, so the colours were garish and very bright. The batteries in the remote were fading, so it was difficult to adjust but we got used to it and found something we could watch. Geoff had brought a bottle of wine back with him when he had gone out. I only had one glass.

That night, after meeting Geoff's sister, I felt tired and went to bed earlier than Geoff. I read for a while but must have dozed off, the book slipping from my hand. That is not unusual for me. I stirred in my sleep and the book fell to the floor, landing with a thud that brought me back to wakefulness. I gazed around me, wondering for a moment where I was, as you sometimes do in a strange place. I was still groggy with sleep. I am not sure what time it was or how long I had been in bed. As I found my bearings, I began to feel the weight of a presence nearby, the consciousness of being observed. I looked up and saw Geoff standing at the open door to my bedroom. As my eyes adjusted, his figure came in to focus. He was just wearing his boxer shorts, ready for bed. There was only the small bedside lamp on in my bedroom. The kitchen or bathroom light might have been on or it could have been moonlight or streetlight through the thin curtains but I discerned a slight glow in the corridor that connected the bedrooms. I could see Geoff's outline highlighted in the doorway, and then could see Geoff's face more clearly as I concentrated on him. Our eyes locked for a moment. He did not stir. I might have pulled the covers a little higher on my chest, feeling a chill, though there was still a little, residual heat from the hot water bottle near my feet. Geoff did not move but kept his gaze fixed on me. It can hardly have been more than a minute on from the first moment that I noticed him standing there.

"Goodnight," he said, eventually, and I said the same to him.

Geoff closed my door and I rolled over to go back to sleep. Despite the chill and the unfamiliar surroundings and the not especially comfortable bed, I slept well that night. There was something soothing, enveloping, in the thought of Geoff and the dogs sleeping under the same roof, nearby, just a few feet away from me.

We stayed at Geoff's mother's house for four nights in total. Some order was beginning to emerge when we left if only measured by the number of black bags and packed boxes piled around the house, the full bins and the empty shelves. I think Geoff might have initially planned to stay a few more days but the task began to get to him. As it turned out, we did not see Ellie again on our visit, and I did not meet her husband or her son whilst we were there. Another time perhaps. I think I began to see before Geoff did that only small inroads into the task of clearing the house could be made on that visit. I knew, and Geoff surely knew, that the appetite for disposing of the belongings of a loved one soon fails you. It has too much sentiment attached to it, to go at it full tilt for long.

"I've had enough," Geoff said, finally, "I'll have to come back or let Ellie do some next. There's no rush, I suppose. Some of this can wait now until the house is sold and we have to clear it properly."

"I'm not sure I've been much help to you here," I said.

"Just having your company has been a great help. I think I would have pretty much despaired on the first day if you hadn't been here."

Geoff brought back some kitchen things, tableware, photos. There was not a great deal of room left in the car for him to bring too much extra baggage home with him. When Ellie had been at the house they had sat down together and they each had taken a few items that must have had special resonance for each of them. The next time I was at Geoff's house, I noticed the green vase on the mantelpiece. It looked well there.

Since returning, something feels different, something feels disrupted. I find the time stretching out until my next meeting with Geoff. The habits and structures I have installed in my life since Yvonne died don't quite seem enough to keep me busy and occupied for a whole day now. I pace about a bit, I can't settle. I sit on the sofa switching channels, nothing sustaining my attention for long. Points of familiarity in my life have changed and I haven't quite caught up with those changes and adjusted to them. I am going round to Geoff's for dinner tonight and tomorrow we are going to the cinema again. Geoff hasn't told me yet what we are going to see but he seems keen to keep a flow of contact between us and we have to make plans to maintain that, organise things and make arrangements. We will run out of things to do, I imagine. It will come to the point where we will just have to sit in front of the telly, side by side on the sofa, with the heating on, not saying very much. I would like that.

Spending time with Geoff at the bungalow, I became aware that our lifestyles did not always gel; the times we tend to eat, the times we went to bed. Try as I might, I couldn't stay up much beyond nine o'clock at night. Zeno was ready for her bed at about the same time. Not that I was sleepy, just that my concentration started to wander. I rarely go straight to sleep when I go to bed. I read and think maybe. But my body kept its regular clock ticking, Zeno's too, and it felt not quite right to fight it too vigorously in those few days. Geoff was not too long after me, when I went to bed, though I suspect that like Yvonne, he could stay up into the wee hours, in his own home. When you are retired, you can do this and why wouldn't you really? Just let the natural rhythm of your body take over, vary your bedtime, tune into the flow of the seasons, sleep when it gets dark, eat when you get hungry. I don't think I am quite ready to give nature that sort of leeway, however, probably never will be.

During our stay under the roof of Geoff's parents, with the ghosts of their lives still around us, we did begin to move our habits and routines closer together, asserting a sort of confederacy against an alien atmosphere. Without any detailed discussion about it, we began to accommodate each other's ways and worked well together as a team, tackling jobs in tandem, harmonising our schedules and customs. With Yvonne, there was a stricter division of labour and allocation of tasks. If one of us cooked, the other stayed out of it until the meal was placed on the table. With Geoff, I found we worked around and with each other. If he peeled the potatoes, I washed the carrots. If I washed up, he dried. Neither of us sat down in front of the telly until the job was done. Then we sat down together.

On our last night, I read for longer than I usually do. Perhaps I was waiting for Geoff to retire before I could snuggle down to sleep. The bedside lamp was on and I had left my door open, perhaps so that I could see when Geoff retired. Eventually, Geoff came up. He must have gone into his own room and undressed for bed, stripping down to his boxers, before using the bathroom. He paused as he passed my door and I put my book down on the bedclothes.

"What are you reading?" he asked.

I lifted my book and showed him the cover. He came up to the bed and sat beside me, to see the book more clearly but he didn't comment and did not look at the book too closely. I could see that he was shivering a bit, goose-bumped on the arms. For some reason, the heating did not work so well in the bedrooms and they were colder than the rest of the house. Some people prefer a cooler bedroom and it might have been designed that way. I didn't like to see him out in the cold so I pulled back the corner of the covers to let Geoff in. No need for him to freeze. I shuffled over a little and Geoff slipped in beside me. He asked me about the book and we talked a little. I put the book down and Geoff suddenly seemed very close to me. I was conscious of his breathing, the heat from him, his bare chest. Calmly, he arose towards me and we kissed.

I have to say it that way, accept it that way. He did not kiss me. We kissed each other. Geoff's arms were around me, his hands moved across my body, over my tee-shirt. Everything happened slowly, nothing was rushed or forced. After just a few moments, Geoff relaxed back onto the pillow. He did not push anything beyond a limit comfortable to me, though I could tell when he pressed himself close to me that the signal of his readiness was there on Geoff's body.

Geoff smiled.

"I'll leave you to get some sleep," he said, "we'll set off back first thing if you like."

I nodded. He kissed me briefly again and we said goodnight.

I didn't pick up my book again that night. I turned off the light but it must have been another twenty minutes or so before I fell asleep.

I had very little left to pack, for our trip back. I set my alarm.

Spring is well embedded now. It has been a very mild start to the year. Since we returned from Geoff's mother's house, there has been no snow, only the occasional frosty morning and always weak sunshine that occasionally beams stronger and warmer. The year has seemed eager to turn, to bring back warmth and light and shake off the dark, cold months.

I have kept up with the garden this past year, not letting leaves accumulate, pruning as far as my expertise takes me, keeping things tidy. It hasn't been a hardship or something to put off. I have enjoyed seeing the spring bulbs peeping through and showing their colours. There seem to be more daffodils this year than I remember, more tulips coming through. Perhaps it is just a good year for them or perhaps I did something right last year to let them flourish. I think I will bring more colour into the garden this summer also; bedding plants, a few shrubs, nothing that needs a lot of tending, nothing that limits Zeno's enjoyment of the space, just odd spots of interest here and there. I might invest in some garden furniture too. One year, maybe, I will install a greenhouse and try to grow a few vegetables. It all adds interest to life, I think.

Geoff is here most days or I am at his house. He calls for me at home in the morning or I will call for him at his home, to have our walk with the girls. We stay in each other's company when we return, have lunch together, go out somewhere perhaps, plan activities for the days following. We go to the gym together now. We have even shopped together. I have lost any anxiety about cooking for Geoff if he comes for dinner. He knows my style of cooking and my limitations. Still, we tend to eat more at Geoff's house than we do at mine. He has toned down the spice in his food. It's no longer an occasion when we eat together, just part of what we do. Sometimes I don't even bother to tidy up when Geoff comes over.

Geoff's neighbours have come to know me and we exchange a few words when I see them. I find I am a bit more outward-looking than I was, less buried down in myself. On my walks with Zeno, on our walks out with Geoff and Bella, we stop and chat with people, more than I did in the past. I have got to know people's names. Just little things like that, I notice.

I have not stayed the night at Geoff's house or he, at mine. We sleep in our own beds.

Geoff has been over to his mother's house on several occasions since the time we went there together. He does the journey always in one day, does not stay overnight. He hasn't suggested I go with him. I don't think I would want to go back. Maybe I feel it has served its purpose and it would be just a chore now. Geoff's sister has taken over the direction of the work to clear the house but Geoff helps out. The house is on the market. It looks well enough in the photographs in the estate agent's details and the signs are that it should sell quickly. His mother appears to be on her last legs now. I think Geoff will be glad when everything is resolved and he can move on.

Geoff is all for making plans in anticipation of this. He has talked about going on holiday together, perhaps abroad, when all the business with his mother is concluded. He wants to see some of those places he never got to with Jim, whilst he is still fit enough to enjoy it. With Jim, their holidays were always to a coastal destination and with Jim's academic interests, these holidays often ended up more of a field trip. This left many of the world's most beautiful or fascinating places unexplored. Cities like Paris and Rome, mountains, lakes, whole countries even. Should I go? He doesn't want to go alone. It wouldn't be the same. I know it would mean leaving Zeno and Bella behind. Could she bear that? Could I bear it? Zeno would fret or so I assume but I have never really left her for a long stretch of time or overnight. Zeno and Bella would be kennelled together, I suppose. It might not be an issue. Geoff says that Bella has stayed in kennels before and did not seem traumatised by it. We could acclimatise them to it by degrees; a weekend away somewhere to start with. I think I could share a room with Geoff. Maybe I need to acclimatise to that; twin beds in a shared room. I think I could admit that degree of intimacy.

Some days, Geoff proceeds as if we have already agreed it between us to take a holiday together. It just needs us to fix a date and place. I have not committed to anything so far. I haven't really said anything about his proposals. But I must say that idea of travelling, and farther afield at that, appeals to me, and sooner rather than later. It's a big world and life is short.

From this big world, I have had an unexpected communication today. I received a letter in the post from my sister, Barbara, in Australia. It must be a couple of years since I last heard from her, and then no more than a Christmas card, I expect. I have not seen her since our mother's funeral. She didn't bring her husband then, left him at home looking after their two sons. Can't remember when I last saw them. I wouldn't recognise them or her husband, Gordon, I suspect, if I saw them on the street. Barbara did send photographs with her letter. I'm not sure when they were taken. The boys were close to manhood, by the looks of it. They all looked very blonde, fit, tanned and better-looking than I remembered. A tan can help with that, I know. It all seemed many miles away, geographically and metaphorically, from our northern town beginnings.

It was quite a long letter. There was years' worth of news to pass on, I suppose. Barbara had not been well but was now apparently fully recovered. Times like that do make you think of family, the wider circle. She regretted that we had not stayed in touch and asked if I was well. She knew that Yvonne had passed and hoped I was doing all right. Then she came to the crux of the matter. Her eldest boy was going to get married towards the end of the year and she wanted me to come over to Australia for it. Make it a long stay, a holiday, catch up. I could stay with her or if I wanted a bit of privacy she could find me somewhere local where I could stay. They would take me about the place, show me the local area but I should take the opportunity to explore further afield whilst I was there. It is a beautiful country.

I have thought of Barbara from time to time over the past few years but felt their life was pretty much complete without me and if she had wanted to stay in touch, she would have done. Obviously, I now realise that the distance that has developed between us is as much down to me as her. Maybe I thought I was the one whose life was complete. I see now that my life was curtailed rather than complete. If I truly wanted to reconnect more with the outside world, then reconnecting with Barbara seemed to me a great test of my resolve in this matter. I find that I do want to see her. And I want to go to Australia. And I want Geoff to come too.

Of course, Barbara knows nothing of Geoff but she left space in her invitation (Or so I read it), to include someone else, on the remote chance I expect that another person might have gained a small foothold in my life. It was most probably a polite gesture, made in acknowledgement of a possibility rather than with any strong sense of its likelihood. I was not going to fret about how I presented what has happened with Geoff; I try not to fret how I present it even to myself. I am sure Barbara will be fine with me bringing a companion.

Travelling is best in company especially on a journey with something of the epic about it.

I have to admit that I have already drafted a letter to Barbara saying that I accept her invitation and that I will be bringing a friend. I will post it on the way over to meet Geoff. Rather recklessly, I haven't even mentioned it to Geoff yet. I will tell him when I see him when the letter will already be in the post. If Geoff can't face it or it isn't convenient, I will go alone. But I think I know him well enough now to take a few things for granted. I didn't want to waste any time at all in replying to Barbara.

Now I am the one thinking of plans and logistics. I know Barbara will look after us when we are there, will help with organising air tickets, connections and such like. Geoff is a seasoned traveller too, from what he tells me. On my own, I wouldn't know where to start. There is the question of Zeno and Bella still. Perhaps Geoff knows someone who could dog-sit. I think that would be less disruptive and unsettling for them, to stay in a familiar place, even without me and Geoff around. I think I have heard that you can hire people to do this. This option would be preferable. There would be little point in a short visit to Australia or even going for just a couple of weeks. A month would be ideal, maybe six weeks, to see something of the country and spend time with Barbara. It is a long time to be away, though. I would miss Zeno enormously.

I will be seeing Geoff very soon and I will tell him all. I can't wait to see his face.

It has been over a year now since Geoff and I first shared breakfast. I noted the anniversary as it passed. It was another of those occasions when I have felt obligated to pause and reflect. There have been quite a few of those moments over the past eighteen months. I have had a lot to think about. It has been a period of change.

Geoff drops hints, perhaps to help me shape my thoughts, perhaps to direct them. He has clearly been reflecting too. He readily welcomed the idea of a trip to Australia. He clearly sees this as a significant milestone, my suggesting it, my including him in a major family event. Perhaps this has encouraged him more than I foresaw and now he wants to have a conversation about where we are and where we go from here. He wants to talk about the future (Thankfully, he doesn't yet say 'our' future).

I don't think I had any sort of mental picture of the 'future' as a concept, a year ago. It was not at the forefront of my mind. I did not visualise it, unless it was as something that just came relentlessly and mercilessly at you, certainly not as something that you could shape or anticipate. Perhaps, if pressed, I would have characterised it as an obscure foreboding of a gradual decline, a fading away to a point of termination. Zeno alone for company. Now I can see that potentially there is a good stretch of time ahead of me. I am older but somehow I don't yet think of myself as old. Why not share that time that is left, long or short as it might be, companionably?

At present, I discourage Geoff from starting that conversation. I think it unnecessary to bring things too much out into the open, things that I believe have already taken and will continue to take their course, without the interference of thought or direction on my part. Perhaps Geoff has more actively steered those things along. However, I tend to think that he was surprised by his feelings too. But what are his feelings? What are my feelings?

I dread Geoff using the words 'taking things further' with all that might imply. But I am equally anxious that Geoff hasn't used those words to me yet and I wonder why he hasn't. There has only been Yvonne in my life, in that way. I cannot conceive of anyone else but I realise that just by speculating along these lines I am conceiving of it and, however vaguely, imagining it, anticipating it. Am I worried about it? Yes, but what worries me is what would worry me with anyone I came close to now, regardless of gender, an unfocused anxiety, being vulnerable, being unsure, a fear of failing in some way, a fear of being hurt or disappointed. But I trust Geoff. He has given me no reason not to trust him.

Geoff proposes that we share a space for a while, see how it goes, see how it suits. Sometimes, he presents this purely in practical terms; convenience, sharing bills, pooling resources. Sometimes, it is something more than this; open-ended, small steps, no promises or commitments at this stage. Either way, I find I have no arguments that form themselves into an objection. All it needs is courage on my part, that tiny push that takes me over the line.

For preference, I would like to stay in my own home, with Geoff and Bella joining me. It is a bigger space, a bigger garden, closer to the sea. If I can keep some of my familiar things about me, keep some part of what I know and value around me, then the things that are different won't seem so challenging, I think.

The days go by and I have pushed my thoughts about for long enough. I have decided to bring this process to a conclusion. I can no longer sustain this restless, meandering state of mind. It could have gone on forever. Once it might have. But I don't want to lose the future through fear and prevarication. I don't want to waste any more time.

As far as I am concerned, it is settled. Now that we have made some sort of plan, however fluid and reversible it might be, I find that I hope that Geoff stays a long while. At last, I will have a reason to clear out Yvonne's side of the wardrobe. I don't think we have to reach too quickly for definitions or conclusions, to give it structure and a name at this stage. I don't know if it is companionship or what it is. I haven't used that other word, that short, ubiquitous word, to describe it. I haven't even said it in my head. I haven't even let Geoff say it. But I feel that what is meant to happen, will happen.

Perhaps this is a point where I stop analysing everything too deeply, just accept and welcome.

I can see Geoff at the door. He won't knock. He knows I have seen him. The door is on the latch anyway. I can see through the glass panel in the door that he has brought a large suitcase and Bella is with him.

There is nothing else to say.